Return To Promise

Dear Friends,

As with any project, there are a number of people to whom I owe my appreciation. The first on the list this time is my editor, Paula Eykelhof, who can be credited with the idea of bringing my readers back to Promise. The minute Paula made the suggestion, I knew she was right. Everywhere I went people were telling me they wanted more, more, more about Promise. Readers told me that the friends they'd made there were like family—and they wanted an update. And so, *Return to Promise* started taking shape in my mind.

I also want to express my thanks to Irene, Nancy, Renate, Jenny and everyone who makes up my Dream Team. Every writer should be so fortunate as to work with such a terrific group of women.

While I have your attention, let me direct you to the dedication page. *Return to Promise* is dedicated to Ruthanne Devlin, a local bookseller and dear friend. Ruthanne understands my addiction to books and does her best to feed it. This dedication is her birthday gift. Not only that, the day I gave it to her just happened to be my birthday, and the very day my granddaughter Maddy was born. Ruthanne, her sister, Sandy, and I were going out to lunch to observe our shared October birthdays when Jenny went into labor with Maddy. It's not a day I'm likely to forget!

If this is your first visit to Promise, a small ranching town in the Texas Hill Country, I promise you're going to enjoy meeting the people there. If this is a return trip, sit back and say howdy to your friends. They've been looking forward to filling you in about what's been happening in their lives....

Debbie Macomber

DEBBIE MACOMBER

Return To Promise

MIRA®

ISBN 1-55166-613-8

RETURN TO PROMISE

Copyright © 2000 by Debbie Macomber.

All rights reserved. Except for use in any review, the reproduction or
utilization of this work in whole or in part in any form by any electronic,
mechanical or other means, now known or hereafter invented, including
xerography, photocopying and recording, or in any information storage or
retrieval system, is forbidden without the written permission of the publisher,
MIRA Books, 225 Duncan Mill Road, Don Mills, Ontario, Canada M3B 3K9.

All characters in this book have no existence outside the imagination of the
author and have no relation whatsoever to anyone bearing the same name
or names. They are not even distantly inspired by any individual known or
unknown to the author, and all incidents are pure invention.

MIRA and the Star Colophon are trademarks used under license and registered
in Australia, New Zealand, Philippines, United States Patent and Trademark
Office and in other countries.

Visit us at www.mirabooks.com

Printed in U.S.A.

To
Ruthanne Devlin
For blessing my life with
your friendship
Happy Birthday 1999

Chapter 1

Cal Patterson knew his wife would be furious when she learned what he'd done. Competing in the annual Labor Day rodeo, however, was worth Jane's wrath—although very little else was.

Bull riding had always enticed him, even more than bronc riding or roping or any of the other competitions. It was the thrill that got to him, the danger of riding a fifteen-hundred-pound bull, of staying on for eight seconds and sometimes longer. He craved the illusion that for those brief moments he was in control. Cal didn't do it for the trophy—if he was fortunate enough to take top prize—or to hear his name broadcast across the rodeo grounds. He was drawn by the challenge, pitting his will against the bull's savage strength, and yes, the risk. Jane would never understand that; she'd been raised a city girl and trained as a doctor, and she disapproved of what she called unnecessary risk. He'd tried to explain his feelings about bull riding, but clearly he'd failed. Jane still objected fervently whenever he mentioned his desire to enter rodeo competitions. Okay, okay, so he'd busted a rib a few years back and spent several pain-filled weeks recuperating. Jane had been angry with him then, too. She'd gotten over it and she would again—but not without inducing a certain amount of guilt first.

He watched her out of the corner of his eye as she ushered their three-year-old son, Paul, into the bleachers. Cal dutifully followed behind, carrying eighteen-month-old Mary Ann, who was sound asleep in his arms. As soon as his family was settled, he'd be joining the other competitors near the arena. A few minutes later, Jane would open the program and find his name. Once she did, all hell would break loose. He sighed heavily. His brother and sister-in-law would be arriving shortly, and if he was lucky, that'd buy him a couple of minutes.

"Glen and Ellie are meeting us here, aren't they?" Jane asked, her voice lowered so as not to disturb the baby. His daughter rested her head of soft blond curls against his shoulder, thumb in her mouth. She looked peaceful, downright angelic—

which was quite a contrast to her usual energetic behavior.

"They'll be here soon," Cal answered, handing Mary Ann to Jane.

With two children demanding her time and attention, plus the ranch house and everything else, Jane had cut back her hours at the medical clinic to one weekend a month. Cal knew she missed practicing medicine on a more frequent basis, but she'd never complained. He considered himself a fortunate man to have married a woman so committed to family. Once the kids were in school, she'd return to full-time practice, but for now, Paul and Mary Ann were the focus of her life.

Just then, Jane reached for the schedule of rodeo events and Cal tensed, anticipating her reaction.

"Cal Patterson, you *didn't!*" Her voice rose to something resembling a shriek. She turned and glared at him, her beautiful face contorted in a look of exasperated disbelief.

"Cal?" She waited, apparently hoping for an explanation.

However, he had nothing to say that he hadn't already said dozens of times. It wouldn't do any good to trot out his rationalizations yet again; one look told him she wouldn't be easily appeased. His only option was to throw himself on her good graces and pray she'd forgive him quickly.

"You signed up for the *bull ride?*"

"Honey, now listen—"

"Are you *crazy?* You got hurt before! What makes you think you won't get hurt this time, too?"

"If you'd give me a chance to—"

Jane stood, cradling Mary Ann against her. Paul stared at his parents with a puzzled frown.

"Where are you going?" he asked, trying to come up with some way to mollify her without causing a scene.

"I don't intend to watch."

"But, darling…"

She scowled at him. "Don't you darling me!"

Cal stood, too, and was given a reprieve when Glen and Ellie arrived, making their way down the long, narrow row of seats. His brother paused, glancing from one to the other, and seemed to realized what was happening. "I take it Jane found out?"

"You knew?"

Ellie shook her head. "Not me! I just heard about it myself."

"Looks like Jane's leaving me," Cal joked, hoping to inject some humor into the situation. His wife was overreacting. There wasn't a single reason she should walk out now, especially when she knew how excited their three-year-old son was about seeing his first rodeo.

"That's exactly what you deserve," she muttered, bending to pick up her purse and the diaper bag while holding Mary Ann tightly against her shoulder.

"Mommy?"

"Gather your things," she instructed Paul. "We're going home."

Paul's lower lip started to quiver, and Cal could tell that his son was trying valiantly not to cry. "I want to see the rodeo."

"Jane, let's talk about this," Cal pleaded.

Paul looked expectantly from his father to his mother, and Jane hesitated.

"Honey, please," Cal said, hoping to talk her into forgiveness—or at least acceptance. Okay, so he'd kept the fact that he'd signed up for the bull riding a secret, but only because he'd been intent on delaying a fight.

"I don't want Paul to see you injured," she argued.

"Have a little faith, would you?"

His wife frowned, her anger simmering.

"I rode bulls for years without a problem. Tell her, Glen," he said, nodding at his brother.

"Hey," Glen said, raising both hands in a gesture of surrender. "You're on your own with this one, big brother."

"I don't blame you for being mad," Ellie said, siding with Jane. "I'd be furious, too."

Women tended to stick together, but despite Ellie's support, Cal could see that Jane was weakening.

"Let Paul stay for the rodeo, okay?" he cajoled. "He's been looking forward to it all week. If you don't want him to see me compete, I understand. Just leave when the bull riding starts. I'll meet you at the chili cook-off once I'm finished."

"Please, Mommy? I want to see the rodeo," Paul said again, eyes huge with longing. The boy pleaded his case far more eloquently than *he* could, and Cal wasn't fool enough to add anything more.

Jane nodded reluctantly, and with a scowl in his direction, she sat down. Cal vowed he'd make it up to her later.

"I'll be fine," he assured her, wanting Jane to know he loved and appreciated her. He slid his arm around her shoulders and gave a gentle squeeze. But all the while, his heart thundered with excitement at the thought of getting on the back of that bull. He couldn't keep his gaze from wandering to the chute.

Jane might have been born and raised in the big city, but she was more than a little bit country now. Still, she'd probably never approve of certain rodeo events. Cal recognized her fears, and as a result, rarely competed anymore—hadn't in five years. But he expected Jane to recognize the impulses that drove him, too. Compromise. Wasn't that what kept a marriage intact?

Jane had no intention of forgetting Cal's deceit, but now wasn't the time or place to have it out with her husband. He knew how she felt about his competing in the rodeo. She'd made her views completely clear, even before they were married.

Still, Jane had acquiesced and held her tongue. She glanced at Cal's brother and sister-in-law and envied them. Their kids were with a baby-sitter, since they planned to attend the dance later that evening. Jane would've preferred to stay herself, but when she'd mentioned it to Cal, he'd balked. Dancing wasn't his favorite activity and he'd protested and complained until she dropped it.

Then he'd pulled *this* stunt. Men!

Partway through the rodeo, Paul fell asleep, leaning against her side. Cal had already left to wait down by the arena with the other amateur riders. As the time approached for him to compete, she considered leaving, but then decided to stay. Her stomach would be in knots whether she was there watching him or not. Out of sight wasn't going to put her risk-taking husband out of her mind, and with Paul asleep, there was no reason to go now.

"Are you worried?" Ellie asked, casting her a sympathetic look.

"Damn straight. I don't know what Cal was thinking." He had more to lose than ever, and to risk injury for no practical purpose was beyond her comprehension.

"Who said he was thinking at all?" Ellie teased.

"Yeah—it's the testosterone," Jane muttered, wondering what her husband found so appealing about riding such dangerous beasts. Her nerves were shattered, and that wasn't going to change. Not until she knew he was safe.

"I was hoping you and Cal would come to the dance."

Ellie was obviously disappointed, but no more than Jane herself. She would have loved an evening out. Had she pressed the issue, Cal would eventually have given in, but it hadn't seemed worth the arguments and the guilt. Besides, getting a sitter would've been difficult, since nearly everyone in Promise attended the annual Labor Day rodeo—and Ellie had managed to snag the services of Emma Bishop, one of the few teenagers available for baby-sitting.

"Cal didn't want to leave the kids," she explained. There would be other dances, other opportunities, Jane reassured herself.

"He's up next," Glen said.

"Go, Cal!" Ellie squealed. Despite her sister-in-law's effort to sound sympathetic, Jane could tell she was truly excited.

Sure enough, Cal's name was announced. Jane didn't want to look, but she couldn't stop herself. Cal was inside the pen, sitting astride the bull, one end of a rope wrapped around the saddle horn and the other around his hand. She held her sleeping child more tightly and bit her lower lip hard enough to draw blood. Suddenly the gate flew open and fifteen hundred pounds of angry bull charged into the arena.

Almost immediately, Glen and Ellie were on their feet, shouting. Jane remained seated, her arms around her children. "What's happening, what's happening?" she asked Ellie.

"Cal's doing great!" she exclaimed. Jane could barely hear her over the noise of the crowd. Ellie clapped wildly when the buzzer went. "He stayed on!" she said proudly.

Jane nodded. How he'd managed to last those eight seconds, she had no idea.

"Whew. Glad that's over." Ellie sank down next to Jane.

"My brother's got a real flair for this," Glen said to no one in particular. "He could have gone on the circuit if..." He let the rest fade.

"If he wasn't married," Jane said, completing his thought. Actually Glen's assessment wasn't really accurate. Her husband was a long-established rancher before she'd come on the scene. He'd competed in rodeos since he was in his teens, but if he'd been interested in turning professional, he would have done so when he was much younger. She had nothing to do with that decision.

"Glen," Ellie said, squeezing her husband's arm, "who's that woman over there?" Ellie was staring at a brunette standing near the fence.

"What woman?" Glen asked.

"The one talking to Cal."

Jane glanced over, and even from this distance she could see that the other woman was lovely. Tall and slender, she looked like a model from the pages of a Western-wear catalog in her tight jeans, red cowboy boots and brightly checked shirt. It was more than just her appearance, though. Jane noticed the confidence with which she held herself, the flirtatious way she flipped back her long brown hair. This was a woman who knew she looked good—particularly to men.

"She seems familiar," Ellie said, nudging Glen. "Don't you think?"

"She does," he agreed, "but I can't place her."

"She's apparently got a lot to say to Cal," Ellie added, then glanced apologetically toward Jane as though she regretted mentioning it.

Jane couldn't help being curious. The woman wasn't anyone she recognized. Normally she wasn't the jealous type, wasn't now, but she found herself wondering how this Rodeo Princess knew her husband. Even from this distance, it was clear that the woman was speaking animatedly to Cal, gesturing freely. For his part, Cal seemed more interested in what was happening with the rodeo than in listening to her.

Jane supposed she should be pleased by his lack

of interest in another woman, and indeed she was. Then, as if aware of her scrutiny, her husband turned toward the bleachers and surveyed the crowd. His face broke into a wide grin when he caught her eye, and he waved. Earlier she'd been annoyed with him—in fact, she still was—but she'd never been able to resist one of Cal's smiles. She waved in return and blew him a kiss.

An hour later, after Cal had been awarded the trophy for the amateur bull-riding competition, they decided to leave. With Mary Ann in the stroller and Paul walking between them, they made one last circuit of the grounds before heading toward the parking lot. They passed the chili cook-off tent, where the winner's name was posted; for the first time in recent memory, it wasn't Nell Grant. But then, Jane understood that Nell had declined to enter this year.

It was near dusk and the lights from carnival rides sparkled, delighting both Paul and Mary Ann. Cal's arm was around Jane's shoulder as they skirted the area set aside for the dance. The fiddle players were entertaining the audience while the rest of the musicians set up their equipment. People had gathered around, tapping their feet in anticipation.

The lively music had Jane swaying to the beat.

"I wish we were staying," she murmured, swallowing her disappointment.

"We'd better get home," Cal said, swinging his trophy at his side. "I didn't want to say anything before, but I'm about as sore as a man can get."

"Your rib?" she asked.

He nodded. "Are you going to lecture me?"

"I should," she muttered. "But I won't. You knew the risks."

He leaned forward and kissed her cheek. "You're right. I did."

What really bothered her was that he'd known— and participated, anyway. He was fully aware that he could have been badly injured, or worse. And for what? She simply didn't understand why a man would do anything so foolish when he had so much to lose.

"I'm ready to go home," he said. "How about you?"

Jane nodded, but glanced longingly over her shoulder at the dance floor. Maybe next year.

The phone rang, shattering the night silence. Cal bolted upright and looked at the glowing digital numbers of the clock radio, then snatched the receiver from its cradle. It went without saying that anyone phoning at 3:23 a.m. was calling with bad news.

"Pattersons'," he barked gruffly.

"Cal? It's Stephanie."

Jane's mother. Something was very wrong; he could hear it in her voice. "What's happened?"

"It's...it's Harry," she stammered.

Jane awoke and leaned across the bed to turn on the bedside lamp. "Who is it?" she asked.

He raised one hand to defer her question. "Where are you?"

"At the hospital," Stephanie said, and rattled off the name of a medical facility in Southern California. "Harry's fallen—he got up the way he sometimes does in the middle of the night and...and he slipped."

"Is he all right?"

"No," his mother-in-law answered, her voice trembling. She took a moment to compose herself. "That's why I'm calling. His hip's broken and apparently it's a very bad break. He's sedated and scheduled for surgery first thing in the morning, but...but the doctors told me it's going to take weeks before he's back on his feet."

"Cal?" Jane was watching him, frowning, her hair disheveled, her face marked by sleep.

"It's your mother," he said, placing his hand over the mouthpiece.

"Is this about my dad?"

Cal nodded.

"Let me talk to her," Jane demanded, instantly alert.

"Stephanie, you'd better talk to Jane yourself," he said, and handed his wife the phone.

Cal was pretty much able to follow the conversation from that point. With her medical background, Jane was the best person to talk to in circumstances like this. She asked a number of questions concerning medication and tests that had been done, explained the kind of orthopedic surgery her dad would undergo and reassured her mother. She spoke with such confidence that Cal felt his own sense of foreboding diminish. And then she hesitated.

"I'll need to talk to Cal about that," she told her mother, voice dropping as though he wasn't supposed to hear.

"Talk to me about what?" he asked after she'd replaced the receiver.

Jane paused for a moment, then took a deep breath.

"Mom wants me and the kids to fly home."

"For how long?" The question was purely selfish; still, he needed to know. Being separated would be a hardship on them all. He understood the situation and was willing to do whatever he could, but he didn't like the thought of their being apart for any length of time.

"I don't know. A couple of weeks, maybe longer."

"Two weeks?" He hated the telltale irritation in his voice, but it was too late to take back his words.

Jane said nothing. Then, as though struck by some brilliant idea, she scrambled onto her knees and a slow smile spread across her face.

"Come with us," she said urgently.

"To California? Now?" That was out of the question, but he hated to refuse his wife—especially after this business with the rodeo. "Honey, I can't. Glen and I are getting ready for the bull sale this week. I'm sorry, but this just isn't a good time for me to be away."

"Glen could handle the sale."

What she said was true, but the prospect of spending two weeks at his inlaws' held little appeal. Cal got along with Jane's mother and he liked her father well enough, but Harry had a few annoying mannerisms. The two of them tended to become embroiled in ridiculous arguments that served no real purpose and usually went nowhere. Cal suspected it was more a matter of their competing for Jane's attention. Jane was Harry's only daughter and he doted on her. Cal figured he'd be doing Harry a favor by staying away. Besides, what would he do with himself in a place like Los Angeles?

"Don't be so quick to say no," she pleaded. "We could make this a family vacation. We always talk about going somewhere and it just never happens." She knew he found it difficult to leave the Lonesome Coyote Ranch for longer than a few days, but this was as good a time as any.

"A vacation? I don't think so, not with your father laid up and your mother as worried as she is. Besides, Stephanie doesn't want *me* there."

"That's not true."

"It's not me she needs, it's you. Having the kids around will boost your father's spirits, and your mother's too. Whereas I'll just be in the way."

Jane's disappointment was obvious. "You're sure?"

He nodded. "You go. A visit with you and the kids will be the best thing for both your parents, and you'll have time to connect with your friends, too. It'll do everyone good.''

Still Jane showed reluctance. ''You're *sure* you don't mind me being gone that long?''

''I'll hate it,'' he admitted, and reached for the lamp to turn off the light. Then he lay back down and drew his wife into his arms.

Jane released a deep sigh. ''I'm going to hate it, too.''

Cal closed his eyes, already experiencing a sense of loss, and Jane and the children hadn't even left yet.

The next morning was hectic. The minute she got up, Jane arranged the flight to California and threw clothes, toiletries, toys and baby supplies into several suitcases. No sooner had she finished than Cal piled them all into the car, and drove his family to San Antonio. Paul was excited about riding in an airplane, and even Mary Ann seemed to realize there was adventure ahead.

As always, San Antonio International Airport was bustling with activity, and after checking them in with the airline, Cal quickly ushered Jane and the kids to their gate, where the flight was already boarding.

Kneeling down to meet his son at eye level, Cal

put both hands on Paul's shoulders. "You be good for Mommy, understand?"

His three-year-old nodded solemnly, then tossed his small arms around Cal's neck, hugging him fiercely.

"I'm counting on you to be as much help to your grandma and grandpa as you can," Cal added. He felt a wrenching in his stomach. This would be the first time he'd been apart from his children.

"I will," Paul promised.

Cal noted that his son's "blankey" was tucked inside his backpack, but said nothing. The blanket was badly worn. It'd been a gift from Jane's friend Annie Porter, and a point of contention between him and Jane. Cal didn't like the idea of the boy dragging it around, and Jane felt that Paul would give it up when he was ready.

Cal stood and scooped Mary Ann into his arms. His daughter squirmed, eager to break free and explore this wonderful new place. It was probably a good thing they didn't have a lot of time for farewells, he reflected unhappily.

"I'll phone often," Jane said after he kissed her.

"Do." Saying goodbye to his family was even more difficult than Cal had anticipated.

The four of them moved toward the jetway,

slowed down by the children's pace and Jane's carry-on luggage.

"I'm going to miss you," he murmured as they reached the airline representative who collected the boarding passes.

"Two weeks will go quickly."

"Right," Cal agreed, but at the moment those weeks loomed before him in all their emptiness.

Juggling two bags and clutching both children, Jane disappeared into the jetway. Had it been anyone else, Cal would have left then, his duty completed, but he stood at the window and waited until the plane had taxied toward the runway. The feeling of emptiness stayed with him, growing. Deep in his gut, he recognized that he'd let his wife down. He should have gone with her; it was what she'd wanted, what she'd asked of him, but he'd refused. He shook his head miserably. This wasn't the first time he'd disappointed Jane.

As he turned toward the parking garage, Cal couldn't shake his reaction to seeing his wife leave. He didn't want to go to California, and yet he regretted not being on that plane with his family.

"You heard about Jane, didn't you?" Dovie Hennessey asked her husband. Frank had just come home from the golf course, where he'd played eighteen holes with Phil Patterson, Cal's father.

Frank, who'd retired three years earlier from his position as sheriff, nodded and made straight for the refrigerator. "According to Phil, Cal drove Jane and the kids to the airport yesterday morning."

"I give him a week."

Frank turned around, a pitcher of iced tea in his hand. "A week before what?"

"Before Cal heads into town."

"Why?"

Exasperated, Dovie rolled her eyes. "Company. He's going to rattle around that house like a lost soul."

"Cal? No way!" Frank argued, pouring himself a tall glass of tea. "You seem to forget he was a confirmed bachelor before he met Jane. I was as surprised as anyone when he decided to marry her. Don't get me wrong. I think it was the smartest thing he ever did...."

"But?" Dovie said.

"Cal isn't any stranger to living alone," Frank continued, sitting down at the kitchen table with his tea and the newspaper. "He did it for years. Now, I know he loves Jane and the kids, but my guess is he's looking forward to two weeks of peace and quiet.''

Dovie couldn't help herself. *Peace and quiet?* Frank made it sound as though Cal would welcome a vacation from his own family. She planted her hands on her hips and glared at her husband. ''Frank Hennessey, what a rotten thing to say.''

He glanced up from his paper, a puzzled expression on his face. ''What was so terrible about that?''

''Jane and the children are *not* a nuisance in Cal's life,'' she said in a firm voice. ''Don't you realize that?''

''Now, Dovie—''

''Furthermore, you seem to imply that he's going to *enjoy* having them gone.''

''I said no such thing,'' Frank insisted. ''Cal's going to miss Jane…of course he is. The children, too. What I was trying to say is that spending a couple of weeks without his wife might not be all that bad.'' Flustered and avoiding her gaze, Frank rubbed his face. ''That didn't come out right, either.''

Dovie suppressed a smile. They'd been married long enough for her to know what he meant, but she liked giving him a hard time once in a while—

partly because he made it so easy. He'd remained a bachelor for the first sixty years of his life. Like Cal, he'd grown accustomed to his own company. He and Dovie had been involved for more than ten years, but Frank had resisted marriage until Pastor Wade McMillen had offered a viable solution. They became husband and wife but kept their own residences. In the beginning, that had worked beautifully, but as time passed, Frank ended up spending more and more nights with her, until it seemed wasteful to maintain two homes. Since he'd retired, Dovie, who owned an antique store, had reduced her hours, as well. They were traveling frequently now, and with Frank taking a role in local politics and becoming active in the senior citizens' center, why, there just weren't enough hours in a day.

Patting her husband's arm as she passed, Dovie said, "I thought I'd make Cal one of my chicken pot pies and we could take it out to him later this week."

Frank nodded, apparently eager to move away from the subject. "Good idea." Reaching for his paper, he claimed the recliner and stretched out his legs. Almost immediately, Buttons, the small black poodle they'd recently acquired, leaped into Frank's lap and circled a couple of times before settling into a comfortable position.

"Nap time?" Dovie asked with a grin.

"Golf tires me out," Frank said.

"You promised to drive me to the grocery store," she reminded him, although she was perfectly capable of making the trip on her own. It was the small things they did together that she enjoyed most. The small domestic chores that were part of any marriage.

"In a while," Frank said sleepily, lowering the newspaper to the floor.

True to his word, an hour later Frank sought her out, apparently ready to tackle a trip to the supermarket. Once they arrived, he found a convenient parking spot, mentioned her offer to make a meal for Cal and grabbed a cart. Dovie marched toward the produce aisle, with Frank close behind.

"Do you have any idea what Cal would enjoy with the pot pie?" she asked.

"I know what *I'd* enjoy," Frank teased, and playfully swatted her backside.

"Frank Hennessey," Dovie protested, but not too loudly; that would only encourage him. She didn't really mind, though. Frank was openly affectionate, unlike her first husband. Marvin had loved her, she never doubted that, but had displayed his feelings in less obvious ways.

"Who's that?" Frank asked, his attention on a tall brunette who stood by the oranges, examining them closely.

It took Dovie a moment to remember. "Why, that's Nicole Nelson."

"Nicole Nelson," Frank repeated slowly, as though testing the name. "She's from Promise?"

"She lived here a few years back," Dovie said, taking a plastic bag and choosing the freshest-looking bunch of celery.

"How do I know her?" Frank asked, speaking into her ear.

Which told Dovie that Nicole had never crossed the law. Frank had perfect recall of everyone he'd encountered in his work as sheriff.

"She was a teller at the bank."

"When?"

"Oh, my." Dovie had to think about that one. "A number of years ago now...nine, maybe ten. She was roommates with Jennifer Healy."

"Healy. Healy. Why is that name familiar?"

Dovie whirled around, sighing loudly. "Frank, don't tell me you've forgotten Jennifer Healy!"

He stared back at her, his expression blank.

"She's the one who dumped Cal two days before their wedding. It nearly destroyed the poor boy. I still remember how upset Mary was having to call everyone and tell them the wedding had been canceled." She shook her head. "Nicole was supposed to be her maid of honor."

Frank's gaze followed the other woman as she pushed her cart toward the vegetables. "When Jennifer left town, did Nicole go with her?"

Dovie didn't know, but it seemed to her the two girls had moved around the same time.

"Cal was pretty broken up when Jennifer dumped him," Frank said. "Good thing she left Promise. Wonder why this one came back…"

"Mary was worried sick about Cal," Dovie murmured, missing her dearest friend more than ever. Cal's mother had died almost three years ago, and not a day passed that Dovie didn't think of her in one way or another.

"I know it was painful at the time, but Jennifer's leaving was probably a lucky break."

Dovie agreed with him. "I'm sure Jane thinks so, too."

Frank generally didn't pay much attention to other women. His noticing Nicole was unusual enough, but it was the intensity of his focus that perturbed her.

She studied Nicole. Dovie had to admit that the years had been good to Jennifer's friend. Nicole had been lovely before, but immature. Time had seasoned her beauty and given her an air of casual sophistication. Even the way she dressed had changed. Her hair, too.

"She's a real looker," Frank commented.

Dovie saw that her husband wasn't the only man with his eye on this woman; half the men in the store noticed her—and Nicole was well aware of it.

"I'll admit she looks attractive," Dovie said with a certain reluctance.

Frank turned back to her. She didn't realize right away that he was frowning. "What is it?" she asked.

"What she looks like to me," he said, ushering her down the aisle, "is trouble."

Chapter 2

Cal had lived in this ranch house his entire life, and the place had never seemed as big or as empty as it did now. Jane hadn't been gone a week and already the silence was driving him to wander aimlessly from room to room. Exhausted from a day that had started before dawn, he'd come home and once again experienced a sharp pang of loneliness.

Normally when Cal got back to the house, Paul rushed outside to greet him. The little boy always launched himself off the porch steps into his father's waiting arms as if he'd waited for this moment the entire day. Later, after Cal had showered and Jane dealt with getting dinner on the table, he spent time with his daughter. As young as Mary Ann was, she already had a dynamic personality and persuasive powers to match. Cal knew she was going to be a beauty when she grew up—and he'd be warding off boys. Mary Ann was like her mother in her loveliness, energy…and her stubborn nature.

Cal's life had changed forever the day he married Jane. Marriage was more than the smartest move of his life; it was the most comfortable. Being temporarily on his own made him appreciate what he had. He'd gotten used to a great many things, most of which he hadn't stopped to consider for a long time: shared passion, the gentle companionship of the woman he loved, a family that gave him a sense of purpose and belonging. In addition, Jane ran their household with efficiency and competence, and he'd grown used to the work she did for her family—meals, laundry, cleaning. He sighed. To say he missed Jane and the kids was an understatement.

He showered, changed clothes and dragged himself into the kitchen. His lunch had been skimpy and his stomach felt hollow, but he wasn't in the mood to cook. Had there been time before she left, Jane would have filled the freezer with precooked dinners he could pop into the microwave. When they heard he was a temporary bachelor, Frank and Dovie had dropped off a meal, but that was long gone. The cupboards were full, the refrigerator, too, but nothing seemed easy or appealing. Because he didn't want to bother with anything more complicated, he reached for a bag of microwave popcorn. That would take the edge off his hunger, he decided. Maybe later he'd feel like putting together a proper meal.

The scent of popped corn enticed him, but just as he was about to start eating it, the phone rang. Cal grabbed the receiver instantly, thinking it might be Jane.

"Pattersons'," he said eagerly.

"Cal, it's Annie."

Annie. Cal couldn't squelch the letdown feeling that settled over him. Annie Porter was his wife's best friend and a woman he liked very much. She'd moved to Promise a few years back and had quickly become part of the community. The town had needed a bookstore and Annie had needed Promise. It wasn't long before she'd married the local vet. Cal vaguely recalled Jane asking him to phone Annie. He'd forgotten.

"I just heard about Jane's dad. What happened? Dovie was in and mentioned that Jane went to stay with her parents—she assumed I knew. I wish someone had told me."

"That's my fault," Cal said. "I'm sorry, Annie.

On the way to the airport, Jane asked me to call...''
He let his words drift off.

"What happened?" Annie asked again, clearly upset. Cal knew she was close to Jane's parents and considered them a second family.

Cal told her everything he could and apologized a second time for not contacting her earlier. He hoped Annie would see that the slight hadn't been intentional; the fact was, he hated to make phone calls. Always had.

"I can't imagine why Jane hasn't called me herself," she said in a worried voice.

Cal had assumed she would, too, which only went to show how hectic Jane's days must be with her parents and the children.

"Jane will be home in a week," Cal said, trying to sound hopeful and reassuring—although a week seemed like an eternity. He pushed the thought from his mind and forced himself to focus on their reunion. "Why don't you give her a call?" he suggested, knowing Annie was going to want more details. "She'd love to hear from you, I'm sure."

"I'll do that."

"Great... Well, it's been good talking to you," he said, anxious to get off the phone.

"Before we hang up, I want to ask you about Nicole Nelson."

"Who?" Cal had no idea who she was talking about.

"You don't know Nicole? She came into the bookstore this afternoon and applied for a job. She put you and the bank down as references."

"Nicole Nelson," he repeated. The name sounded vaguely familiar.

"I saw you talking to her at the rodeo," Annie said, obviously surprised that he didn't remember the other woman.

"Oh, yeah—her," he said, finally recalling the incident. Then he realized how he knew Nicole. She'd been a good friend of Jennifer's. In fact, they'd been roommates at the time he and Jennifer were engaged. "She put my name down as a job reference?" He found that hard to believe.

"She said she's known you for a number of years," Annie added.

"Really?" To be fair, Cal's problem hadn't been with Nicole but with Jennifer, who'd played him for a fool. He'd been too blinded by his first encounter with love to notice the kind of woman she was.

"Nicole said if I had any questions I should ask you."

"It's been years since I saw her—other than at the rodeo last week." He did remember talking to her briefly. She'd said something about how good it was to be back in Promise, how nice to see him, that sort of thing. At the time Cal had been distracted. He'd been more interested in watching the rodeo and cheering on his friends than in having a conversation with a woman he'd had trouble recognizing. Besides, Jane was upset with him and appeasing her had been paramount. He'd barely noticed Nicole.

"Did she list any other personal references?" he asked.

"No, I told her you and the bank were the only ones I needed," Annie continued. "So you do remember her?"

"Sure. It's just that it was a long time ago."

"You went out with her?"

Leave it to Annie to ask a question like that. "No, with her best friend. We almost got married." No need to go into details. Jennifer had taught him one of the most valuable lessons of his life. The worth of that experience could be measured in the pain and embarrassment that resulted when she'd callously canceled the wedding. He could've lived with her breaking their engagement—but why did she have to wait till they were practically at the altar?

"I talked with Janice over at Promise First National about her job history," Annie said, interrupting his thoughts. "She doesn't have anything negative to say about Nicole, but if you're uncomfortable giving her a recommendation…"

"Oh, I'm sure Nicole will do a great job for you."

The length of Annie's hesitation told him he hadn't been very convincing.

"Nicole's fine, really," he added. He didn't actually remember that much about her. She always seemed to be there whenever he picked up Jennifer, but he couldn't say he knew her. Years ago she'd been a sweet kid, but that was the extent of his recollection. He couldn't dredge up anything that would prevent her from selling books. He'd never heard that she was dishonest or rude to customers, and those were things that would definitely have stuck in his mind. It was difficult enough to attract good employees; Cal didn't want to be responsible for Annie's not hiring someone simply because he had negative feelings about that person's friends.

"I was thinking of hiring her for the bookstore."

"Do," Cal urged.

"She seems friendly and helpful."

"I'm sure she is," Cal said, and glanced long-ingly toward the popcorn.

"Thanks, Cal, I appreciate the input."

"No problem." He didn't know what it was about women and the telephone. Even Jane, who had a sensible approach to everything and hated wasting time, could spend hours chatting with her friends. Just thinking about his wife produced a powerful yearning. Nothing seemed right without her.

"I'll give Jane a call later," Annie was saying.

"Good plan." He checked his watch, wondering how much longer this would take.

"Thanks again."

"Give Nicole my best," he said, thinking this was how to signal that he was ready to get off the phone.

"I will," Annie promised. "Bye, now."

Ah, success. Cal replaced the receiver, then frowned as he attempted to picture Nicole Nelson. Brown hair—or blond? He hadn't paid much atten-tion to her at the rodeo. And he couldn't imagine what would bring her back to Promise. Not that she needed to justify the move, at least to him. His one hope was that he didn't give Annie reason to regret hiring her.

* * *

Mary Ann's squeal of delight woke Jane from a deep sleep. She rolled over and looked bleary-eyed at the clock radio and gasped. Ten o'clock. She hadn't slept that late since she was in high school. Tossing aside the covers, she reached for her robe and headed out of the bedroom, yawning as she went.

"Mom!" she called.

"In here, sweetheart," her mother said from the kitchen.

Jane found the children and her mother busily playing on the tile floor. Mary Ann toddled gleefully, chasing a beach ball, intent on getting to it before her brother. Because he loved his little sister, Paul was letting her reach it first, then clapping and encouraging her to throw it to him.

"You should have woken me up," Jane said.

"Why? The children are fine."

"But, Mom, I'm supposed to be here to help you," she protested. The last week had been hectic. Taking Paul and Mary Ann away from home and the comfort of their normal routine had made both children difficult and irritable. That first night, Mary Ann hadn't slept more than a few hours, then whined all the next day. Paul had grown quiet and refused to talk to either grandparent. The children had required several days to adjust to the time change, and with the stress of her father's condition, Jane was completely exhausted.

"You needed the sleep," her mother said.

Jane couldn't argue with that. "But I didn't come all this way to spend the whole morning in bed."

"Stop fussing. Paul, Mary Ann and I are having a wonderful time. If you intend to spoil it, then I suggest you go back to bed."

"Mother!"

"I'm the only grandma they have. Now, why don't you let us play and get yourself some breakfast?"

"But—"

"You heard me." Stephanie crawled toward the lower cupboards, then held on to the counter, using that as leverage to get up off the floor. "I'm not as limber as I once was," she joked.

"Oh, Mom…" Watching her, Jane felt guilty. She gathered Mary Ann into her arms, although the child immediately wanted down. Paul looked up at her, disgruntled by the interruption.

"Your father's resting comfortably," her mother informed her. "He wants us to take the day for ourselves."

"Dad said that?" He'd been demanding and impatient ever since Jane had arrived.

"He did indeed, and I intend to take him up on his offer. I promised the kids lunch at Mc-Donald's."

"Dad *must* be feeling better."

"He is," her mother said. "By the way, Annie phoned earlier."

"Annie?" Jane echoed. "Is everything all right at home?"

"Everything's just fine. She wanted to know how your father's doing. Apparently no one told her—"

"I asked Cal to let her know. I meant to phone her myself, but…you know how crazy it's been this last week."

"I explained it all, so don't you worry. She'd already talked to Cal, who apologized profusely. She sounds well and has some news herself."

Jane paused, waiting, although she had her suspicions.

"Annie's pregnant again. Apparently they're all thrilled—Annie, Lucas and the children. She's reducing her hours at work, hiring extra help. It was great to chat with her."

"A baby. That's wonderful." Annie was such a good mother, patient and intuitive. And such a good friend. Her move to Texas had been a real blessing to Jane.

Just thinking about Promise made Jane's heart

hunger for home. A smile came as she recalled how out of place she'd once felt in the small Texas town. She'd accepted a job in the medical clinic soon after she'd qualified. It wasn't where she'd hoped to settle, and she'd only taken the assignment as a means of paying off a portion of her huge college loans. The first few months had been dreadful—until she'd become friends with Dovie, who'd introduced her to Ellie.

This was networking at its finest. Soon afterward, Ellie and Glen had arranged Jane's first date with Cal. What a disaster that had been! Cal wasn't the least bit interested in a blind date. Things had quickly changed, however, when Cal and his brother and Ellie had started to teach her how to think and act like a real Texan. When she'd decided to take riding lessons, Cal had volunteered to be her teacher.

Jane had never meant to fall in love with him. But they were a good match, bringing out the best in each other, and they'd both recognized that. Because of Cal, she was a better person, even a better physician, and he reminded her often how her love had enriched his life. They were married within the year.

After the children arrived, Jane felt it necessary to make her career less of a priority, but she didn't begrudge a moment of this new experience. In fact, she enjoyed being a full-time wife and mother—for a while—and managed to keep up her medical skills with part-time work.

Annie, too, had found love and happiness in their small town. The news of this pregnancy pleased Jane.

"Have you connected with Julie and Megan yet?" her mother asked.

Along with Annie, Julie and Megan had been Jane's best friends all through high school. Julie was married and lived just ten minutes away. Megan was a divorced single mother. Jane hadn't seen either woman in three years—make that four. How quickly time got away from her.

"Not yet," Jane told her.

"I want you to have lunch with your friends while you're home."

"Mom, that isn't necessary. I'm not here to be entertained."

"I don't want you to argue with me, either."

Jane grinned, sorely tempted to follow her mother's suggestion. Why not? she decided. She'd love to see her friends. "I'll try to set something up with Julie this week."

"Good." Her mother gently stroked Jane's cheek. "You're pale and exhausted."

The comment brought tears to her eyes. *She* wasn't the one suffering pain and trauma, like her father, who'd broken his hip, or her mother who'd been left to deal with the paramedics, the hospital, the surgeon and all the stress.

"I came here to help *you*," Jane reiterated.

"You have, don't you see?" Her mother hugged Paul. "It's time with my precious grandbabies that's helping me deal with all this. I don't see nearly enough of them. Having the grandkids with me is a rare treat, and I fully intend to take advantage of it."

Jane headed for the shower, looking forward to visiting with her friends. She missed Cal and Promise, but it was good to be in California, too.

The metallic whine of the can opener made Cal grit his teeth. This was the third night in a row that he'd eaten soup and crackers for dinner. The one night he'd fried himself a steak, he'd overcooked it. A few years back he'd been a pretty decent cook, but his skills had gotten rusty since his marriage. He dumped the ready-to-heat soup into the pan and stared at it, finding it utterly unappetizing.

Naturally he could always invite himself to his brother's house for dinner. Glen and Ellie would gladly set an extra plate at their table. He'd do that when he got desperate, but he wasn't, at least not yet. For that matter, he could call his father. Phil would welcome the company, but by the time Cal was finished with his chores on the ranch and showered, dinner had already been served at the seniors' center.

Actually, now that he thought about it, he was in the mood for Mexican food, and no place served it better than Promise's own Mexican Lindo. Already his mouth was watering for his favorite enchiladas, dripping with melted cheese. He could almost taste them. Needing no other incentive, he set the soup, pan and all directly inside the refrigerator and grabbed his hat.

If he hurried, he decided, he'd be back in time for Jane's phone call. Her spirits had seemed better these past few days. Her father was improving, and today she'd met a couple of high-school friends for lunch.

Soon Harry would be released from the hospital, and once his father-in-law was home, Jane and the children would return to Texas. Cal sincerely wished Jane's father a speedy recovery—and his good wishes weren't entirely selfish. He liked Harry Dickinson, despite their arguments and despite his father-in-law's reservations about Jane's choice in a husband. He'd never come right out and said anything, but Cal knew. It was impossible not to. Still, Harry's attitude had gotten a bit friendlier, especially after the children were born.

Promise was bustling when Cal drove up Main Street. All the activity surprised him, although it shouldn't have. It was a Thursday night, after all, and there'd been strong economic growth in the past few years. New businesses abounded, an area on the outskirts of town had been made into a golf course, and the city park had added a year-round swimming pool. Ellie's feed store had been remodeled, but it remained the friendly place it'd always been. She'd kept the wooden rockers out front and his own father was among the retired men who met there to talk politics or play a game of chess. The tall white steeple of the church showed prominently in the distance. Cal reflected that it'd been a long time since he'd attended services. Life just seemed to get in the way. Too bad, because he genuinely enjoyed Wade McMillen's sermons.

The familiar tantalizing aroma of Texas barbecue from the Chili Pepper teased his nostrils, and for a moment Cal hesitated. He could do with a thick barbecue sandwich just as easily as his favorite enchiladas, but in the end he stuck with his original decision.

When he walked into the stucco-walled restaurant, he was immediately led to a booth. He'd barely had time to remove his hat before the waitress brought him a bowl of corn chips and a dish of extra-hot salsa. His mouth was full when Nicole Nelson stepped into the room, eyed him boldly and smiled. After only the slightest pause, she approached his table.

"Hello, Cal." Her voice was low and throaty.

Cal quickly swallowed the chip, almost choking as he did so. The attractive woman standing there wasn't the kid he'd known all those years ago. Her jeans fit her like a second skin, and unless he missed his guess, her blouse was one of those designer numbers that cost more than he took to the bank in an average month. If her tastes ran to expensive clothes like that, Cal couldn't imagine how she intended to live on the amount of money Annie Porter could afford to pay her.

"Nicole," he managed. "Uh, hi. How're you doing?"

"Great, thanks." She peered over her shoulder as though expecting to meet someone. "Do you have a couple of minutes?"

"Uh...sure." He glanced around, grateful no one was watching.

Before he realized what she intended, Nicole slid

into the booth opposite him. Her smile was bright enough to make him blink.

"I can't *tell* you how good it is to see you again," she said, sounding genuine.

"You, too," he muttered, although if he'd passed her in the street, he probably wouldn't have recognized her.

"I imagine you're surprised I'm back in Promise."

"Yeah," he said. "What brings you to town?" He already knew she'd made the move without having a job lined up.

She reached for a chip, then shrugged. "A number of reasons. The year I lived in Promise was one of the best of my life. I really did grow to love this town. Jennifer and I got transferred here around the same time, but she never felt about Promise the way I did."

"Jennifer," he said aloud. Cal couldn't help wondering what had become of his ex-fiancée. "Are you still in touch with her?"

"Oh, sure. We were best friends for a lot of years."

"How is she?"

"Good," Nicole told him, offering no details.

"Did she ever marry?" He was a fool for asking, but he wanted to know.

Nicole dipped the chip in his salsa and laughed lightly. "She's been married twice."

"Twice?" Cal could believe it. "Last I heard she was living with a computer salesman in Houston." He'd heard that from Glen, who'd heard it from Ellie, who'd heard it from Janice at the bank.

"She married him first, but they've been divorced longer than they were ever married."

"I'm sorry to hear that." He wasn't really, but it seemed like something he should say.

"Then she met Mick. It wasn't his real name, but she called him that because he was from Australia."

"Why Mick?"

"Mick Dundee."

"Oh," he said, and remembered that was a character in a popular movie from the 1980s.

"Jennifer thought Mick was hot stuff," Nicole continued. "They had a whirlwind courtship, married in Vegas and divorced a year later."

"I imagine she was upset about that," Cal said, mainly because he didn't know how else to comment.

"With Jennifer it's hard to tell," Nicole said, leaning forward.

The waitress approached the table and Nicole declined a menu, but asked for a strawberry margarita.

"Actually I'm meeting someone later, but I saw you and I thought this was a good opportunity to catch up on old times."

"Sure." Not that they'd *had* any "old times." Then, because he wasn't sure she realized he was married, he added, "I could use the company. My wife and kids are in California with her family for the next week or so."

"Oh..."

He might have been wrong, but Cal thought he detected a note of disappointment in her voice. Surely she'd known he was married. Annie must have said something. But then again, perhaps not.

"My boy is three and my daughter's eighteen months."

"Congratulations."

"Thanks," Cal said, feeling a bit self-conscious about dragging Jane and his kids into the conversation. But it was the right thing to do—and it wouldn't hurt his ego if the information got back to Jennifer, either.

Nicole helped herself to another chip. "The last time Jennifer and I spoke, she said something that might interest you." Nicole loaded the chip with salsa and took a discreet nibble. Looking up, she widened her eyes. "Jen said she's always wondered what would've happened if she'd stayed in Promise and you two *had* gotten married.''

Cal laughed. He knew the answer, even if Nicole and Jennifer didn't. ''I simply would've been husband number one. Eventually she would have moved on.'' In retrospect, it was easy to see Jennifer's faults and appreciate anew the fact that they weren't married.

''I don't agree,'' Nicole said, surprising him. ''I think it might have been a different story if she'd stayed with you.''

The waitress brought her drink and Nicole smiled her thanks. She took a sip, sliding her tongue along the salty edge of the glass. ''Jennifer might be my best friend,'' she went on, ''but when it comes to men she's not very smart. Take you, for example. I couldn't *believe* it when she told me she was calling off the wedding. Time has proved me right, too.''

Cal enjoyed hearing it, but wanted to know her reasoning. ''Why's that?''

''Well, it's obvious, don't you think? You were the only man strong enough to deal with her personality. I'm very fond of Jennifer, don't get me wrong, but she likes things her own way and that includes relationships. She was an idiot to break it off with you.''

"Actually it was fortunate for both of us that she did."

"Fortunate for you, you mean," Nicole said with a deep sigh. "Like I said, Jennifer was a fool, and if she doesn't realize it, I do." After another sip, she leaned toward him, her tone confiding. "I doubt she'd admit it, but ever since she left Promise, Jennifer's been looking for a man just like you."

"You think so?" Her remark was a boost to his ego and superficial though that was, Cal couldn't restrain a smile.

The waitress returned with his order, and Nicole drank more of her margarita, then said, "I'll leave you now and let you have your dinner."

She started to slip out of the booth, but Cal stopped her. "There's no need to rush off." He wasn't in any hurry, and he had to admit he liked hearing what she had to say about Jennifer. If he missed Jane's call, he could always phone her back.

Nicole smiled. "I wanted to thank you, too," she murmured.

"For what?" He cut into an enchilada with his fork and glanced up.

"For giving me a recommendation at Tumbleweed Books."

"Hey," he said, grinning at her. "No problem."

"Annie called me this morning and said I have the job."

"That's great."

"I'm thrilled. I've always loved books and I look forward to working with Annie."

He should probably mention that the bookstore owner was Jane's best friend, and would have, but he was too busy chewing and swallowing—and after that, it was too late.

Nicole checked her watch. "I'd better be going. Like I said, I'm meeting a...friend. If you don't mind, I'd like to buy your dinner."

Her words took him by surprise. He couldn't imagine what had prompted the offer.

"As a thank-you for the job reference," she explained.

He brushed aside her offer. "It was nothing—I was glad to do it. I'll get my own meal. But let me pay for your drink."

She agreed, they chatted a few more minutes, and then Nicole left. She hadn't said whom she was meeting, and although he was mildly curious, Cal didn't ask.

He sauntered out of the restaurant not long after Nicole. He'd been dragging when he arrived, but with his belly full and his spirits high, he felt almost cocky as he walked toward his parked truck. He supposed he was sorry to hear about Jennifer's marital troubles—but not *very* sorry.

As it happened, Cal did miss Jane's phone call, but was quick to reach her once he got home and had listened to her message. She sounded disappointed, anxious, emotionally drained.

"Where were you?" she asked curtly when he returned her call.

Cal cleared his throat. "I drove into town for dinner. Is everything okay?"

"Mexican Lindo, right?" she asked, answering one question and avoiding the other.

"Right."

"Did you eat alone?"

"Of course." There was Nicole Nelson, but she hadn't joined him, not technically. Not for dinner, at any rate. He'd bought her drink, but he didn't want to go into lengthy explanations that could only lead to misunderstanding. Perhaps it was wrong not to say something about her being there, but he didn't want to waste these precious minutes answering irrelevant questions. Jane was sure to feel slighted or suspicious, and she had no reason. At any rate, Annie would probably mention that she'd hired Nicole on his recommendation. He could deal with that later. Right now, he wanted to know why she felt upset.

"You'd better tell me what's wrong," Cal urged softly, dismissing the thought of Nicole as easily as if he'd never seen her. Their twenty minutes together had been trivial, essentially meaningless. Not a man-woman thing at all but a pandering to his ego. Jane was his wife, the person who mattered to him.

"Dad didn't have a good day," Jane said after a moment. "He's in a lot of pain and he's cranky with me and Mom. A few tests came back and, well, it's too early to say, but I didn't like what I saw."

"He'll be home soon?"

"I don't know—I'd thought, no, I'd hoped..." She let the rest fade.

"Don't worry about it, sweetheart. Take as long as you need. I'll manage." It wasn't easy to make the offer, but Cal could see that his wife needed his support. These weeks apart were as hard on her as they were on him. This was the only way he could think to help.

"You *want* me to stay longer?" Jane demanded.

"No," he returned emphatically. "I thought I was being noble and wonderful."

The tension eased with her laugh. "You seem to be getting along far too well without me."

"That isn't true! I miss you something fierce."

"I miss you, too," Jane said with a deep sigh.

"How did lunch go with your friends?" he asked, thinking it might be a good idea to change the subject.

"All right," she said with no real enthusiasm.

"You didn't enjoy yourself?"

Jane didn't answer immediately. "Not really. We used to be close, but that seems so long ago now. We've grown apart. Julie's into this beauty-pageant thing for her daughter, and it was all she talked about. Every weekend she travels from one state to another, following the pageants."

"Does her daughter like it?"

"I don't know. It's certainly not something I'd ever impose on *my* daughter." She sighed again. "I don't mean to sound judgmental, but we have so little in common anymore."

"What about Megan?"

"She came with her twelve-year-old daughter and is terribly bitter about her divorce. At every opportunity she dragged her husband's name into the conversation with the preface, 'that bum I was married to.'"

"In front of her kid?" Cal was shocked that any mother could be so insensitive to her child.

"Repeatedly," Jane murmured. "I have to admit I felt depressed after seeing them." She paused, took a deep breath. "I can only imagine what they thought of me."

"That concerns you?" Cal asked, thinking she was being ridiculous if it did.

"Not in the least," Jane was quick to tell him. "Today was a vivid reminder that my home's not in California anymore. It's in Promise with you."

Chapter 3

"I hate to trouble you," Nicole said to Annie. She sat in front of the computer screen in the bookstore office, feeling flustered and impatient with herself. "But I can't seem to find this title under the author's name."

"Here, let me show you how it works," Annie said, sitting down next to Nicole.

Nicole was grateful for Annie Porter's patience. Working in a bookstore was a whole new experience for her. She was tired of banking, tired of working in a field dominated by women but managed by men. Her last job had left her with a bitter taste—not least because she'd had an ill-advised affair with her boss—and she was eager to move on to something completely new. Thus far, she liked the bookstore and the challenge of learning new systems and skills.

Annie carefully reviewed the instructions again. It took Nicole a couple of tries to get it right. ''This shouldn't be so difficult,'' she mumbled. ''I mean, I've worked with lots of computer programs before.''

''You're doing great,'' Annie said, patting Nicole's back.

''I hope so.''

''Hey, I can already see you're going to be an asset to the business,'' Annie said cheerfully, taking the packing slip out of a shipment of books. ''Since you came on board, we've increased our business among young single men by two hundred percent.''

Nicole laughed and wished that was true. She'd dated a handful of times since her return to Promise, but no one interested her as much as Cal Patterson. And he was married, she reminded herself. Married, married, married.

She should have known he wouldn't stay single long. She'd always found Cal attractive, even when he was engaged to Jennifer. However, the reason she'd given him for moving back to Promise was the truth. She had fallen in love with the town. She'd never found anywhere else that felt as comfortable. During a brief stint with the Promise bank, she'd made friends within the community. She loved the down-home feel of Frasier Feed store and the delights of Dovie's Antiques. The bowling alley had been a kick, with the midnight Rock-and-Bowl blast every Saturday night.

Jennifer Healy had never appreciated the town or the people. Her ex-roommate had once joked that living in Promise was one step up from Mayberry RFD. The comment had angered Nicole. These people were sincere, pleasant and kind. *She* preferred life in a town where people cared about each other, even if Jen didn't.

Only it wasn't just the town that had brought her back. Everything she felt about Promise was genuine, but she had another reason. She'd returned because of Cal Patterson.

Almost ten years ago, she'd been infatuated with him, but since her best friend was engaged to him, she couldn't very well do anything about it. Jennifer had dumped him and that would have been the perfect time to stick around and comfort him. Instead, she'd waited—and then she'd been transferred again, to a different branch in another town. Shortly after she'd left Promise, she'd had her first affair, and since then had drifted from one dead-end relationship to another. That was all about to change.

This time she fully intended to claim the prize—Cal Patterson.

At the Mexican restaurant the other night, Nicole had told Cal that since breaking their engagement, Jennifer compared every man she met to him, the one she'd deserted. Nicole hadn't a clue if that was the case or not. *She* was the one who'd done the comparing. In all these years she hadn't been able to get Cal Patterson out of her mind.

So he was married. She'd guessed as much when she made the decision to return to Promise, but dating a married man wasn't exactly unfamiliar to her. She would have preferred if he was single, but she had to admit it—his being married wasn't a deterrent. It only made things more...interesting. More of a challenge. Almost always, the married man ended up staying with his wife, and Nicole was the one who got hurt. This was something she knew far too well, but she'd also discovered that there were ways of undermining a marriage without her having to do much of anything. And when a marriage was shaken, opportunities might present themselves....

"Nicole?"

Nicole realized Annie was staring at her. "Sorry, I got lost in my thoughts."

"It's time for a break." Annie led the way into

the back room. Once inside, she reached for the coffeepot and gestured toward one of two overstuffed chairs. "Sit down and relax. If Louise needs any help, she can call us."

Nicole didn't have to be asked twice. She'd been waiting for a chance to learn more about Cal, and she couldn't think of a better source than Annie Porter.

Annie handed her a coffee in a thick ceramic mug, and Nicole added a teaspoon of sugar, letting it slowly dissolve as she stirred. "How do you know Cal?" she asked, deciding this was the best place to start.

"His wife. You haven't met Jane, have you?"

Nicole shook her head. "Not yet," she said as though she was eager to make the other woman's acquaintance.

"We've been friends nearly our entire lives. Jane's the reason I moved to Promise."

Nicole took a cookie and nibbled daintily. Cal mentioned he has children."

"Two."

"That's what he said." The perfect little family, a boy and a girl. Except that wifey seemed to be staying away far too long. If the marriage was as wonderful as everyone suggested, she would've expected Cal's wife to be home by now.

"This separation has been hard on them."

"They're separated?" Nicole asked, trying to sound sympathetic.

She was forced to squelch a surge of hope when Annie explained, "Oh, no, not that way. Just by distance. Jane's father has been ill."

"Yes, Cal had mentioned that she was in California with her family," Nicole nodded earnestly. "She's a doctor, right?"

"A very capable one. And the fact that she's with her parents seems to reassure them both."

"Oh, I'm sure she's a big help."

"I talked to her mom the other day, who's *so* glad she's there. I talked to Jane, too—I wanted to let her know about the baby and find out about her dad. She's looking forward to getting home."

"I know I'd want to be with my husband," Nicole said, thinking if she was married to Cal, she wouldn't be foolish enough to leave him for weeks at a time. If Jane Patterson was going to abandon her husband, then she deserved what she got.

"The problem is, her father's not doing well," Annie said, then sipped her coffee. She, too, reached for a cookie.

"That's too bad."

Annie sighed. "I'm not sure how soon Jane will to be able to come home." She shook her head. "Cal seems at loose ends without his family."

"Poor guy probably doesn't know what to do with himself." Nicole would love to show him, but she'd wait for the right moment.

"Do you like children?" Annie asked her.

"Very much. I hope to have a family one day." Nicole knew her employer was pregnant, so she said what she figured Annie would want to hear. In reality, she herself didn't plan to have children. Nicole was well aware that, unlike Annie, she wouldn't make a good mother. If she was lucky enough to find a man who suited her, she'd make damn sure he didn't have any time on his hands to think about kids—or to be lured away by another woman. Really, it was usually the wife's own fault for not giving her husband the attention he craved.

"I understand you're seeing Brian Longstreet," Annie murmured.

Nicole had to pause to remember when and where she'd last seen Brian. "We had dinner the other night." The evening hadn't been especially memorable. It was Brian's misfortune to meet her after she'd run into Cal at the Mexican Lindo. Afterward, Cal was all Nicole could think about.

"Do you like him?"

Nicole shrugged. "Brian's okay."

"A little on the dull side?"

"A little." She'd already decided not to date the manager of the grocery store again. He was engaging enough and not unattractive, but he lacked the *presence* she was looking for. The strength of character. His biggest fault, Nicole readily admitted, was that he wasn't Cal Patterson.

"What about Lane Moser?"

Nicole had dated him the first week she'd returned. She'd known him from her days at the bank. "Too old," she muttered. She didn't mind a few years' difference, but Lane was eighteen years her senior and divorced. Besides, if he did any checking on her, he might learn a few things best left undiscovered. And he was just the type to check. "I'm picky," she joked.

"You have a right to be."

"I never seem to go for the guys who happen to be available. I don't know what my problem is," Nicole said, and even as she spoke she recognized this for a bald-faced lie. Her problem was easily defined. Repeatedly she fell for married men; actually she preferred them. It was the challenge, the chase, the contest. Single guys stumbled all over themselves to make an impression, whereas with married men, *she* was the one who had to lure them, had to work to attract their attention.

Over the years she'd gotten smart, and this time it wouldn't be the wife who won. It would be her.

"Don't give up," Annie said, breaking into her thoughts.

"Give up?"

"On finding the right man. He's out there. I was divorced when I met Lucas and I had no intention of ever marrying again. It's all too easy to let negative experiences sour your perspective. Don't let that happen to you."

"I won't," Nicole promised, and struggled to hide a smile. "I'm sure there's someone out there for me—only he doesn't know it yet." But Cal would find out soon enough.

"We'd better get back," Annie said, glancing at her watch.

Nicole set aside her mug and stood. Cal had been on his own for nearly two weeks now, if her calculations were correct. A man could get lonely after that much time without a woman.

He hadn't let her pay for his meal the other night.

Maybe she could come up with another way to demonstrate just how grateful she was for the job recommendation.

"How long did Jane say she was going to be away?" Glen asked Cal as they drove along the fence line. The bed of the pickup was filled with posts and wire and tools; they'd been examining their fencing, doing necessary repairs, all afternoon.

Cal didn't want to think about his wife or about their strained telephone conversations of the last few nights. Yesterday he'd hung up depressed and anxious when Jane told him she wouldn't be home as soon as she'd hoped. Apparently Harry Dickinson's broken hip had triggered a number of other medical concerns. Just when it seemed his hip was healing nicely, the doctors discovered a spot on his lung. It'd shown up earlier, but in the weeks since he'd been admitted, the spot had grown. All at once the big *C* loomed over Jane's father. *Cancer.*

"I don't know when she'll be back," Cal muttered, preferring not to discuss the subject with his brother. Cal blamed himself for their uncomfortable conversation. He'd tried to be helpful, reassuring, but hadn't been able to prevent his disappointment from surfacing. He'd expected her home any day, and now it seemed she was going to be delayed yet again.

"Are you thinking of flying to California yourself?" his brother asked.

"No." Cal's response was flat.

"Why not?"

"I don't see that it'd do any good." He believed that her parents had become emotionally dependent on her, as though it was within Jane's power to take their problems away. She loved her parents and he knew she felt torn between their needs and his. And here he was, putting pressure on her, as well.

He didn't mean to add to her troubles, but he had.

"Do you think I'm an irrational jerk?"

"Yes," Glen said, "so what's your point?"

That made Cal smile. Leave it to his younger brother to say exactly what he needed to hear. "You'd be a lot more sympathetic if it was *your* wife."

"Probably," Glen agreed.

Normally Cal kept his affairs to himself, but he wasn't sure about the current situation. After Jane had hung up, Cal had battled the urge to call her back, settle matters. They hadn't fought, not exactly, but they were dissatisfied with each other. Cal understood how Jane felt, understood her intense desire to support her parents, guide them through this difficult time. But she wasn't an only child— she had a brother living nearby—and even if she had been, her uncle was a doctor, too. The Dickinsons didn't need to rely so heavily on Jane, in Cal's opinion—and he'd made that opinion all too clear.

"What would you do?" Cal asked his brother.

Glen met his look and shrugged. "Getting tired of your own cooking, are you?"

"It's more than that." Cal had hoped Jane would force her brother to take on some of the responsibility.

She hadn't.

Cal and Glen reached the top of the ridge that overlooked the ranch house. "Whose car is that?" Glen asked.

"Where?"

"Parked by the barn."

Cal squinted, and shook his head. "Don't have a clue."

"We'd better find out, don't you think?"

Cal steered the pickup toward the house. As they neared the property, Cal recognized Nicole Nelson lounging on his porch. Her *again?* He groaned in-wardly. Their meeting at the Mexican Lindo had been innocent enough, but he didn't want her mentioning it to his brother. Glen was sure to say something to Ellie, and his sister-in-law would inevitably have a few questions and would probably discuss it with Dovie, and... God only knew where all this would end.

"It's Nicole Nelson," Cal muttered.

"The girl from the rodeo?"

Glen had noticed her that day and oddly Cal hadn't. "You've met her before," he told his brother.

"I have?" Glen sounded doubtful. "When? She doesn't look like anyone I'd forget that easily."

"It was a few years back," Cal said as they approached the house. "She was Jennifer Healy's roommate. She looked different then. Younger or something."

He parked the truck, then climbed out of the cab.

"Hi," Nicole called, stepping down off the porch. "I thought I might have missed you."

"Hi," Cal returned gruffly, wanting her to know he was uncomfortable with her showing up at the ranch like this. "You remember my brother, Glen, don't you?"

"Hello, Glen."

Nicole sparkled with flirtatious warmth and friendliness, and it was hard not to be affected.

"Nicole." Glen touched the rim of his hat. "Good to see you again."

"I brought you dinner," Nicole told Cal as she strolled casually back to her car. She looked as comfortable and nonchalant as anyone he'd ever seen. The way she acted, anyone might think she made a habit of stopping by unannounced.

Glen glanced at him and raised his eyebrows. He didn't need to say a word; Cal knew exactly what he was thinking.

"After everything you've done for me, it was the least I could do," Nicole said. "I really am grateful."

"For what?" Glen looked sharply at Cal, then Nicole.

Nicole opened the passenger door and straightened. "Cal was kind enough to give me a job recommendation for Tumbleweed Books."

"Annie phoned and asked if I knew her," Cal muttered under his breath, minimizing his role.

"I hope you like taco casserole," Nicole said, holding a glass dish with both hands. "I figured something Mexican would be a good bet, since you seem to enjoy it."

"How'd she know that?" Glen asked, glaring at his brother.

"We met at the Mexican Lindo the other night," Cal supplied, figuring the news was better coming from him than Nicole.

"You did, did you?" Glen said, his eyes filled with meaning.

"I tried to buy his dinner," Nicole explained, "but Cal wouldn't let me."

Cal suspected his brother had misread the situation. "We didn't have dinner together if that's what you're thinking," he snapped. He was furious with Glen, as well as Nicole, for putting him in such an awkward position.

Holding the casserole, Nicole headed toward the house.

"I can take it from here," Cal said.

"Oh, it's no problem. I'll put it in the oven for you and get everything started so all you need to do is serve yourself."

She made it appear so reasonable. Unsure how to stop her, Cal stood in the doorway, arms loose at his sides. Dammit, he felt like a fool.

"There's plenty if Glen would like to stay for dinner," Nicole added, smiling at Cal's brother over her shoulder.

"No, thanks," Glen said pointedly, "I've got a wife and family to go home to."

"That's why I'm here," Nicole said, her expression sympathetic. "Cal's wife and children are away, and he's left to fend for himself."

"I don't need anyone cooking meals for me," Cal said, wanting to set her straight. This hadn't been his idea. Bad enough that Nicole had brought his dinner; even worse that she'd arrived when his brother was there to witness it.

"Of course you don't," Nicole agreed. "This is just my way of thanking you for welcoming me home to Promise."

"Are you actually going to let her do this?" Glen asked, following him onto the porch.

Cal hung back. "Dovie brought me some dinner recently," he said, defending himself. "Savannah, too."

"That's a little different, don't you think?"

"No," he snapped. "Nicole's just doing something thoughtful, the same as Dovie and Savannah."

"Yeah, right."

"I'm not going to stand out here and argue with you," Cal muttered, especially since he agreed with his brother and this entire setup made him uncomfortable. If she'd asked his preference, Cal would have told Nicole to forget it. He was perfectly capable of preparing his own meals, even if he had little interest in doing so. He missed Jane's dinners—but it was more than the food.

Cal was lonely. He'd lived by himself for several years and now he'd learned, somewhat to his dismay, that he no longer liked it. At first it'd been the little things he'd missed most—conversation over dinner, saying good-night to his children, sitting quietly with Jane in the evenings. Lately, though, it was everything.

"I'll be leaving," Glen said coldly, letting Cal know once again that he didn't approve of Nicole's being here.

"I'll give you a call later," Cal shouted as Glen got into his truck.

"What for?"

His brother could be mighty dense at times. "Never mind," Cal said, and stepped into the house.

Nicole was already in the kitchen, bustling about, making herself at home. He found he resented that. "I've got the oven preheating to 350 degrees," she said, facing him.

He stood stiffly in the doorway, anxious to send her on her way.

"As soon as the oven's ready, bake it for thirty minutes."

"Great. Thanks."

"Oh, I nearly forgot."

She hurried toward him and it took Cal an instant to realize she wanted out the door. He moved aside, but not quickly enough to avoid having her brush against him. The scent of her perfume reminded him of something Jane might wear. Roses, he guessed. Cal experienced a pang of longing. Not for Nicole, but for his wife. It wasn't right that another woman should walk into their home like this. Dammit, Jane should be here, not Nicole—or anyone else.

"I left the sour cream and salsa in the car," Nicole said breathlessly when she returned. She placed both containers on the table, checked the oven and set the glass dish inside. "Okay," she said, rubbing her palms together. "I think that's everything."

Cal remained standing by the door, wanting nothing so much as to see her go.

She pointed to the oven. "Thirty minutes. Do you need me to write that down?"

He shook his head and didn't offer her an excuse to linger.

"I'll stay if you like and put together a salad."

He shook his head. "I'll be fine."

She smiled sweetly. "In that case, enjoy."

This time when she left, Cal knew to stand far enough aside to avoid any physical contact. He watched her walk back to her car, aware of an overwhelming sense of relief.

Life at the retirement center suited Phil Patterson. He had his own small apartment and didn't need to worry about cooking. The monthly fee included three meals a day. He could choose to eat alone in his room or sit in the dining room if he wanted company. Adjusting to life without Mary hadn't been easy—wasn't easy now—but he kept active and that helped. So did staying in touch with friends. Particularly Frank Hennessey. Gordon Pawling, too. The three men played golf every week.

Frank's wife, Dovie, and Mary had been close for many years, and in some ways Mary's death had been as hard on Dovie as it was on Phil. At the end, when Mary was no longer able to recognize either of them, Phil had sat and wept with his wife's dear friend. He hadn't allowed himself to break down in front of either of his sons, but felt no such compunction when he was around Dovie. She'd cried with him, and their shared grief had meant more than any words she might have said.

Frank and Dovie had Phil to dinner at least once a month, usually on the first Monday. He thought it was a bit odd that Frank had issued an invitation that afternoon when they'd finished playing cards at the seniors' center.

"It's the middle of the month," Phil protested. "I was over at your place just two weeks ago."

"Do you want to come for dinner or not?" Frank said.

Only a fool would turn down one of Dovie's dinners. That woman could cook unlike anyone he knew. Even Mary, who was no slouch when it came to preparing a good meal, had envied Dovie's talent.

"I'll be there," Phil promised, and promptly at five-thirty, he arrived at Frank and Dovie's, a bouquet of autumn flowers in his hand.

"You didn't need to do that," Dovie said when she greeted him, kissing his cheek lightly.

Phil immediately caught a whiff of something wonderful—a blend of delightful aromas. He smelled bread fresh from the oven and a cake of some sort, plus the spicy scent of one of her Cajun specialties.

Frank and Phil settled down in the living room and Dovie soon joined them, carrying an appetizer plate full of luscious little things. A man sure didn't eat this well at the retirement center, he thought. Good thing, too, or he'd be joining the women at their weekly weight-loss group.

Phil helped himself to a shrimp, dipping it in a spicy sauce. Frank opened a bottle of red wine and brought them each a glass.

They chatted amiably for several minutes, but Phil knew something was on Dovie's mind—the same way he always knew when Mary was worried about one thing or another. Phil had an inkling of what it was, too, and decided to break the ice and make it easier for his friends.

''It's times like these that I miss Mary the most,'' he murmured, choosing a brie-and-mushroom concoction next.

''You mean for social get-togethers and such?'' Frank asked.

''Well, yes, those, too,'' Phil said. ''The dinners with friends and all the things we'd planned to do once we retired.''

Dovie and Frank waited.

"I wish Mary were here to talk to Cal."

His friends exchanged glances, and Phil realized he'd been right. They'd heard about Cal and Nicole Nelson.

"You know?" Frank asked.

Phil nodded. It wasn't as though he could *avoid* hearing. Promise, for all its prosperity and growth, remained a small town. The news that Nicole Nelson had delivered dinner to Cal had spread faster than last winter's flu bug. He didn't approve, but he wasn't about to discuss it with Cal, either. Mary could have had a gentle word with their son, and Cal wouldn't have taken offense. But Phil wasn't especially adroit at that kind of conversation. He knew Cal wouldn't appreciate the advice, nor did Phil think it was necessary. His son loved Jane, and that was all there was to it. He'd never do anything to jeopardize his marriage.

"Apparently Nicole brought him dinner—supposedly to thank Cal for some help he recently gave her," Dovie said, her face pinched with disapproval.

"If you ask me, that young woman is trying to stir up trouble," Frank added.

"Maybe so," Phil agreed, but he knew his oldest

son almost as well as he knew himself. Cal hadn't sought out this other woman; she was the one who'd come chasing after him. His son would handle the situation.

"No one's suggesting they're romantically involved," Frank said hastily.

"They aren't," Phil insisted, although he wished again that Mary could speak to Cal, warn him about the perceptions of others. That sort of conversation had been her specialty.

"Do you see Nicole Nelson as a troublemaker?" Phil directed the question to Dovie.

"I don't know... I don't *think* she is, but I do wish she'd shown a bit more discretion. She's young yet—it's understandable."

Phil heard the reluctance in her response and the way she eyed Frank, as though she expected him to leap in and express his opinion.

"Annie seems to like her," Dovie said, "but with this new pregnancy, she's spending less and less time at the bookstore. Really, I hate to say anything...."

"I tell you, the woman's a homewrecker," Frank announced stiffly.

"Now, Frank." Dovie placed her hand on her husband's knee and shook her head.

"Dovie, give me some credit. I was in law enforcement for over thirty years. I recognized that look the minute I saw her."

Phil frowned, now starting to feel seriously worried. "You think Nicole Nelson has set her sights on Cal?"

"I do," Frank stated firmly.

"What an unkind thing to say." Still, Dovie was beginning to doubt her own assessment of Nicole.

"The minute I saw her, I said to Dovie, 'That woman's trouble.'"

"He did," Dovie confirmed, sighing. "He certainly did."

"Mark my words."

"Frank, please," she said, "You're talking as though Cal wasn't a happily married man. We both know he isn't the sort to get involved with a woman like Nicole. With *any* woman. He's a good husband and father."

"Yes," Frank agreed.

"How did you hear about her taking dinner out to Cal?" Phil asked. It worried him that this troublemaker was apparently dropping Cal's name into every conversation, stirring up speculation. Glen was the one who'd mentioned it to Phil—casually, but Phil wasn't fooled. This was his youngest son's way of letting him know he sensed trouble. Phil had weighed his options and decided his advice wasn't necessary. But it seemed that plenty of others had heard about Nicole's little trip to the ranch. Not from Glen and not from Ellie, which meant Nicole herself had been spreading the news. She had to be incredibly naive or just plain stupid or… Phil didn't want to think about what else would be going on in the woman's head. He didn't know her well enough to even guess. Whatever the reason for her actions, if Jane heard about this, there could be problems.

"Glen told Ellie," Dovie said, "and she was the one who mentioned it to me. Not in any gossipy way, mind you, but because she's concerned. She asked what I knew about Nicole." Like Dovie, Ellie didn't want to involve Annie.

"Do you think anyone will say something to Jane?"

Dovie immediately rejected that idea. "Not unless it's Nicole Nelson herself. To do so would be cruel and malicious. I can't think of a single person in Promise who'd purposely hurt Jane. This town loves Dr. Texas." Dr. Texas was what Jane had been affectionately called during her first few years at the clinic.

"The person in danger of getting hurt here is Cal," Frank said gruffly. "Man needs his head examined."

Phil had to grin at that. Frank could be right; perhaps it *was* time to step in, before things got out of hand. "Mary always was better at talking to the boys," he muttered. "But I suppose I'd better have a word with him...."

"You want me to talk to him?" Frank offered.

"Frank!" Dovie snapped.

"*Someone* has to warn him he's playing with fire," Frank blurted, and glanced at Phil, obviously expecting him to agree.

Phil shook his head. "Listen, if anyone says anything, it'll be me."

"You will, won't you?" Frank pressed.

Reluctantly Phil nodded. He would, but he wasn't sure when. Sometimes a situation righted itself without anyone needing to say a word. This just might be one of those cases.

He sincerely hoped so.

Chapter 4

Jane stood at the foot of her father's hospital bed reading his medical chart. Dr. Roth had allowed her to review his notes as a professional courtesy. She frowned as she studied them, then flipped through the test results, liking what they had to say even less.

"Janey? Is it that bad?" her father asked. She'd assumed he was asleep; his question took her by surprise.

Jane quickly set the chart aside. "Sorry if I woke you," she murmured.

He waved off her remark.

"It's bad news, isn't it?" he asked again. "You can tell me, Jane."

His persistence told her how worried he was. "Hmm. It says here you've been making a pest of yourself,'' she said, instead of answering his question.

He shook his head, but wore a sheepish grin. ''How's a man supposed to get any rest around here with people constantly waking him for one thing or another? If I'd known how much blood they were going to draw or how often, I swear I'd make them pay me.'' He paused. ''Do you have any idea what they charge for all this—all these X rays and CAT scans and tests?''

''Don't worry about that, Dad. You have health insurance.'' However, she knew that his real concern wasn't the expense but the other problems that had been discovered as a result of his broken hip.

''I want to know what's going on,'' he said, growing agitated.

''Dad.'' Jane pressed her hand to his shoulder.

He reached for her fingers and squeezed them hard. For a long moment he said nothing. ''Cal wants you home, doesn't he?''

She hesitated, not knowing what to say. Cal had become restive and even a bit demanding; he hadn't hidden his disappointment when she'd told him she couldn't return to Promise yet. Their last few conversations had been terse and had left Jane feeling impatient with her husband—and guilty for reacting that way. In retrospect, she regretted the entire conversation and suspected he did, as well.

"Your mother and I have come to rely on you far too much," her father murmured.

"It's all right," Jane said, uncomfortably aware that Cal had said essentially the same thing. "I'm not only your daughter, I'm a physician. It's only natural that you'd want me here. What's far more important is for you and Mom not to worry."

Her father sighed and closed his eyes. "This isn't fair to you."

"Dad," she said again, more emphatically. "It's all right, really. Cal understands." He might not like it, but he did understand.

"How much time do I have?" he shocked her by asking next. He was looking straight at her. "No one else will tell me the truth. You're the only one I can trust."

Her fingers curled around his and she met his look. "There are very effective treatments—"

"How much time?" he repeated, more loudly.

Jane shook her head.

"You won't tell me?" He sounded hurt, as if she'd somehow betrayed him.

"How do you expect me to answer a question like that?" she demanded. "Do I have a crystal ball or a direct line to God? For all we know, you could outlive me.''

His smile was fleeting. ''All right, give me a ball-park figure.''

Jane was uncomfortable doing even that. ''Dad, you aren't listening to what I'm saying. You're only at the beginning stages of treatment.''

''Apparently my heart isn't in great shape, either.''

What he said was true, but the main concern right now was treating the cancer. He'd already had his first session of chemotherapy, and Jane hoped there'd be immediate results. ''Your heart is fine.''

''Yeah, sure.''

''Dad!''

He made an effort to smile. ''It's a hard thing to face one's failing health—one's mortality.''

When she nodded, he said quietly, ''I worry about your mother without me.''

Jane was worried about her mother, too, but she wasn't about to add to her father's burden. ''Mom will do just fine.''

Her father sighed and looked away. ''You've made me very proud, Jane. I don't think I've ever told you that.''

A lump formed in her throat and she couldn't speak.

"If anything happens to me, I want you to be there for your mother."

"Dad, please, of course I'll help Mom, but don't talk like that. Yes, you've got some medical problems, but they're all treatable. You trust me, don't you?"

He closed his eyes and nodded. "Love you, Janey."

"I love you, too, Dad." On impulse, she leaned forward and kissed his forehead.

"Tell your mother to take the kids to the beach again," he insisted. "Better yet, make that Disneyland."

"She wants to spend the time with you."

"Tell her not to come and visit me today. I need the rest." He opened his eyes and gave her an outrageous wink. "Now get out of here so I can sleep."

"Yes, Daddy," she said, reaching for her purse.

She might be a grown woman with children of her own, but the sick fragile man in that bed would always be the father she loved.

"Mommy, beach?" Paul asked as he walked into the kitchen a couple of mornings later, dragging his beloved blanket behind him. He automatically opened the cupboard door under the counter and checked out the selection of high-sugar breakfast cereals. Her mother had spoiled the children, Jane realized, and it was going to take work to undo that once she was home again.

Home. She felt so torn between her childhood home and her life in Promise, between her parents and her husband. She no longer belonged in California. Texas was in her blood now and she missed it—missed the ranch, her friends...and most of all, she missed Cal.

"Can we go to the beach?" Paul asked again, hugging the box of sugar-frosted cereal to his chest as he carried it to the table.

"Ah..." Her father's doctor was running another set of tests that afternoon.

"Go ahead," her mother urged, entering the kitchen, already dressed for the day. "Nothing's going to happen at the hospital until later."

"But, Mom..." Jane's sole reason for being in California was to help her parents. If she was going to be here, she wanted to feel she was making some contribution to her father's recovery. Since their conversation two days ago, he'd tried to rely on her less, insisting she spend more time with her children. But the fewer demands her father made on her, the more her mother seemed to cling. Any talk of returning to Texas was met with immediate resistance.

"I'll stay with your dad this morning while you go to the beach," her mother said. "Then we can meet at the hospital, and I'll take the children home for their naps."

Jane agreed and Paul gave a small shout of glee. Mary Ann, who was sitting in the high chair, clapped her hands, although she couldn't possibly have known what her brother was celebrating.

"Mom, once we get the final test results, I really need to think about going home. I'm needed back in Promise."

Stephanie Dickinson's smile faded. "I know you are. It's just that it's been so wonderful having you here…"

"I know, but—"

"I can't tell you how much my grandkids have helped me cope with everything that's happening."

"I'm sure that's true." Her mother made it difficult to press the issue. Every time Jane brought up the subject of leaving, Stephanie found an even stronger reason for her to remain "an extra few days.'' Jane had already spent far more time away than she'd intended.

''We'll find out about Dad's test results this afternoon, and if things look okay, I'm booking a flight home.''

Her mother lifted Mary Ann from the high chair and hugged her close. ''Don't worry, honey,'' she said tearfully. ''Your father and I will be just fine.''

''Mother. Are you trying to make me feel guilty?''

Stephanie blinked as if she'd never heard anything more preposterous. ''What a ridiculous thing to suggest! Why would you have any reason to feel guilty?''

Why, indeed. ''I miss my life, Mom—anyway, Derek's here,'' she said, mentioning her younger brother, who to this point had left everything in Jane's hands. Five years younger, Derek was involved in his own life. He worked in the movie industry as an assistant casting director and had a different girlfriend every time Jane saw him. Derek came for brief visits, but it was clear that the emotional aspects of dealing with their parents' situation were beyond him.

''Of course you need to get back,'' her mother

stated calmly as she reached for a bowl and set it on the table for Paul, along with a carton of milk.

The child opened the cereal box and filled his bowl, smiling proudly for having accomplished the feat by himself. Afraid of what would happen if he attempted to pour his own milk, Jane did it for him.

"I want you to brush your teeth as soon as you're finished with your breakfast," she told him. Then, taking Mary Ann with her, she left the kitchen to get ready for a morning at the beach.

Just as she'd hoped, the tests that afternoon showed signs of improvement. Jane was thrilled for more reasons than the obvious. Without discussing it, she called the airline and booked a flight home, then informed her parents as matter-of-factly as possible.

Stephanie Dickinson went out that evening for a meeting with her church women's group—the first social event she'd attended since Harry's accident. A good sign, in her daughter's opinion. Jane welcomed the opportunity to pack her bags and prepare for their return. Paul moped around the bedroom while she waited for a phone call from Cal. She'd promised her son he could speak to his father, but wondered if that had been wise. Paul was already tired and cranky, and since Cal was attending a Cattlemen's Association meeting, he wouldn't be back until late.

"I want to go to the beach again," he said, pouting.

"We will soon," Jane promised. "Aren't you excited about seeing Daddy?"

Paul's lower lip quivered as he nodded. "Can Daddy go to the beach with us?"

"He will one day."

That seemed to appease her son, and Jane got him settled with crayons and a Disney coloring book.

When the phone finally rang, she leaped for it, expecting to hear her husband's voice. Eager to hear it.

"Hello," she said. "Cal?"

"It's me." He sounded reserved, as if he wasn't sure what kind of reception he'd get.

"Hello, you," she said warmly.

"You're coming home?"

"Tomorrow."

"Oh, honey, you don't know what good news that is!"

"I do know. I'll give you the details in a minute. Talk to Paul first, would you?"

"Paul's still up? It's after nine o'clock, your time."

"It's been a long day. I took the kids to the beach this morning and then this afternoon I was at the hospital with my dad when the test results came back." She took a deep breath. "I'll explain later. Here's Paul."

She handed her son the receiver and stepped back while he chatted with his father. The boy described their time at the beach then gave her the receiver again. "Daddy says he wants to talk to you now."

"All right," she said, placing her hand over the mouthpiece. "Give me a kiss good-night and go to bed, okay? We have to get up early tomorrow."

Paul stood on tiptoe and she bent down to receive a loud wet kiss. Not arguing, the boy trotted down the hallway to the bedroom he shared with Mary Ann. Jane waited long enough to make sure he went in.

"I've got the flight information, if you're ready to write it down," she said.

"Yup—pen in hand," Cal told her happily. Hearing the elation in his voice was just the balm she needed.

She read off the flight number and time of arrival, then felt obliged to add, "I know things have been strained between us lately and..."

"I'm sorry, Jane," he said simply. "It's my fault."

"I was about to apologize to you," she said, loving him, anticipating their reunion.

"It's just that I miss you so damn much."

"I've missed you, too." Jane sighed and closed her eyes. They spoke on the phone nearly every night, but lately their conversations had been tainted by the frustration they both felt with their predicament. She'd wanted sympathy and understanding; he'd been looking for the same. They tended to keep their phone calls brief.

"I have a sneaking suspicion your mother's been spoiling the kids."

"She sees them so seldom..." Jane started to offer an excuse, then realized they could deal with the subject of their children's routines later.

"Your dad's tests—how were they?" Cal asked.

"Well, put it this way. His doctors are cautiously optimistic. Dad's coping."

"Your mother, too?"

"Yes." Despite Stephanie's emotional dependence on her, Jane admired the courage her mother had shown in the past few weeks. Seeing her husband in the hospital, learning that he'd been diagnosed with cancer, was a terrifying experience for her. At least, the situation seemed more hopeful now.

"I'll be at the airport ahead of schedule," Cal promised. "Oh, honey, you don't know how good it's going to be to have you back."

"I imagine you're starved for a home-cooked meal," Jane teased.

"It isn't your cooking I miss as much as just having my wife at home," Cal said.

"So you're eating well, are you?"

"I'm eating." From the evasive way he said it, she knew that most of his dinners consisted of something thrown quickly together.

"I'll see you tomorrow," Jane whispered. "At five o'clock."

"Tomorrow at five," Cal echoed, "and that's none too soon."

Jane couldn't agree more.

Cal was in a good mood. By noon, he'd called it quits for the day; ten minutes later he was in the shower. He shaved, slapped on the aftershave Jane preferred and donned a crisp clean shirt. He was ready to leave for San Antonio to pick up his wife and children. His steps lightened as he passed the bedroom, and he realized he'd be sharing the bed with his wife that very night. He hesitated at the sight of the disheveled and twisted sheets. Jane had some kind of obsession with changing the bed linens every week. She'd been away almost three weeks now and he hadn't so much as made the bed. She'd probably appreciate clean sheets.

He stripped the bed and piled the dirty sheets on top of the washer. The laundry-room floor was littered with numerous pairs of mud-caked jeans and everything else he'd dirtied in the time she'd been away. No need to run a load, he figured; Jane liked things done her own way. He'd never known that a woman could be so particular about how the laundry got done.

The kitchen wasn't in terrific shape, either, and Cal regretted not using the dishwasher more often. Until that very moment, he hadn't given the matter of house-cleaning a second thought. He hurriedly straightened the kitchen and wiped down the countertops. Housework had never been his forte, and Jane was a real stickler about order and cleanliness. When he'd lived with his brother, they'd divided the tasks; Cal did most of the cooking and Glen managed the dishes. During the time his wife was away, Cal hadn't done much of either.

Still, he hadn't been *totally* remiss. He'd washed Savannah's and Dovie's dishes. Nicole Nelson's, too. He grabbed his good beige Stetson and started to leave yet again, but changed his mind.

He didn't have a thing to feel guilty about—but sure as hell, if Jane learned that Nicole had brought him a casserole, she'd be upset, particularly since he'd never mentioned it. That might look bad. He hadn't meant to keep it from her, but they'd been sidetracked by other concerns, and then they'd had their little spat. He'd decided just to let it go.

All Cal wanted was his wife and family home. That wasn't so much to ask...especially when he heard about the way she seemed to be spending her days. Just how necessary was it to take the kids to Disneyland? Okay, once, but they'd gone three, maybe four times. He'd lost count of their trips to the beach. This wasn't supposed to be a vacation, dammit. He immediately felt guilty about his lack of generosity. She'd had a lot of responsibility and he shouldn't begrudge her these excursions. Besides, she'd had to entertain the kids *somehow*.

Collecting the clean casserole dishes, Cal stuck them in the back seat of the car. He'd return them right now, rather than risk having Jane find the dish that belonged to Nicole Nelson.

His first stop was at the home of Savannah and Laredo Smith. After some minutes of searching, he found his neighbor in one of her rose gardens, winterizing the plants. They'd grown up living next door to each other, and Savannah's brother, Grady Weston, had been Cal's closest friend his entire life.

Savannah had been piling compost around the base of a rosebush, and she straightened when he pulled into the yard. She'd already started toward him by the time he climbed out of the car.

"Well, hello, Cal," she said, giving him a friendly hug.

"Thought I'd bring back your dish. I want you to know how much I appreciated the meal."

Savannah pressed her forearm against her moist brow. "I was glad to do it. I take it Jane'll be home soon?"

"This afternoon." He glanced at his watch and saw that he still had plenty of time.

"That's wonderful! How's her father doing?"

"Better," he said. He didn't want to go into all the complexities and details right now; he'd leave that for Jane.

"I should go. I've got a couple of other stops to make before I head to the airport."

"Give Jane my best," Savannah said. "Ask her to call me when she's got a minute."

Cal nodded and set off again. His next stop was Dovie and Frank Hennessey's place. Besides a chicken pot pie, Dovie had baked him dessert—an apple pie. It was the best meal he'd eaten the whole time Jane had been in California. Dovie had a special recipe she used for her crust that apparently included buttermilk. She'd passed it on to Jane, but despite several attempts, his wife's pie crust didn't compare with Dovie Hennessey's. But then, no one's did.

Frank answered the door and gave an immediate smile of welcome. "Hey, Cal, good to see you." He held open the back door and Cal stepped inside.

"You, too, Frank." Cal handed him the ceramic pie plate and the casserole dish. "I'm on my way to the airport to pick up Jane and the kids."

"So that's why you're wearing a grin as wide as the Rio Grande."

"Wider," Cal said. "Can't wait to have 'em back."

"Did Phil catch up with you?" Frank asked.

"Dad's looking for me?"

Frank nodded. "Last I heard."

"I guess I should find out what he wants," Cal said. He had enough time, since it was only two o'clock and Jane's flight wasn't due until five. Even if it took him two hours to drive to the airport, he calculated, he should get there before the plane landed. Still, he'd have to keep their visit brief.

Frank nodded; he seemed about to say something else, then apparently changed his mind.

"What?" Cal asked, standing on the porch.

Frank shook his head. "Nothing. This is a matter for you and your dad."

Cal frowned. He had to admit he was curious. If his father had something to talk over with him, Cal wondered why he hadn't just phoned. From Frank and Dovie's house, Cal drove down Elm Street to the seniors' center. He found his father involved in a quiet game of chess with Bob Miller, a retired newspaperman.

"Hello, son," Phil said, raising his eyes from the board.

"Frank Hennessey said you wanted to see me," Cal said abruptly. "Hi, Bob," he added. He hadn't intended any rudeness, but this was all making him a bit nervous.

Phil stared at him. "Frank said that, did he?"

"I brought back Dovie's dishes, and Frank answered the door. If you want to talk to me, Dad, all you need to do is give me a call."

"I know, I know." Phil stood and smiled apologetically at Bob. "I'll be back in a few minutes."

Bob was studying the arrangement of chess pieces. "Take all the time you need," he muttered without looking up.

Phil surveyed the lounge, but there was no privacy to be had. Cal checked his watch, thinking he should preface their conversation with the news that he was on his way to the airport. Before he had a chance to explain why he was in town—and why he couldn't stay long—his father shocked him by saying, "I want to know what's going on between you and Nicole Nelson."

"Nicole Nelson?" Cal echoed.

Phil peered over his shoulder. "Perhaps the best place to have this discussion is my apartment."

"There's nothing to discuss," Cal said, his jaw tightening.

Phil ignored him and marched toward the elevator. "You take back her dinner dishes yet?" he pried. "Or have you advanced to sharing candlelit meals?"

Cal nearly swallowed his tongue. His father

knew Nicole had brought him dinner. How? Glen wasn't one to waste time in idle gossip. Nor was Ellie. He didn't like to think it was common knowledge or that the town was feasting on this nasty tidbit.

His father's apartment consisted of a small living area with his own television and a few bookcases. His mother's old piano took up one corner. Double glass doors led to the bedroom, with a master bath that held both a tub and a shower stall. Although he didn't play the piano, Phil hadn't sold it when Cal's mother died. Instead, he used the old upright to display family photographs.

He walked over to a photo of Cal with Jane and the two children, taken shortly after Mary Ann's birth. "You have a good-looking family, son."

Cal knew his father was using this conversation to lead into whatever nonsense was on his mind. Hard as it was, he bit his tongue.

"It'd be a shame to risk your marriage over a woman like Nicole Nelson."

"Dad, I'm *not* risking my marriage! There's nothing to this rumor. The whole thing's been blown out of proportion. Who told you she'd been out to the ranch?"

"Does it matter?" Phil challenged.

"Is this something folks are talking about?" That was Cal's biggest fear. He didn't want Jane returning to Promise and being subjected to a torrent of malicious gossip.

"I heard the two of you were seen together at the Mexican Lindo, too."

"Dad!" Cal cried, yanking off his hat to ram his fingers through his hair. "It wasn't *like* that. I was eating alone and Nicole happened to be there at the same time."

"She sat with you, didn't she?"

"For a while. She was meeting someone else."

Phil's frown darkened. "She didn't eat with you, but you bought her a drink, right?"

Reluctantly Cal nodded. He'd done nothing wrong; surely his father could see that.

"People saw you and Nicole in the Mexican Lindo. These things get around. Everyone in town knows she brought a meal out to you, but it wasn't Glen or Ellie who told them."

"Then who did?" Even as he asked the question, the answer dawned on Cal. He sank onto the sofa that had once stood in the library of his parents' bed-and-breakfast. "Nicole," he breathed, hardly able to believe she'd do such a thing.

Phil nodded. "Must be. Frank thinks she's looking to make trouble." He paused, frowning slightly. "Dovie doesn't seem to agree. She thinks we're not being fair to Nicole."

"What do *you* think?" Cal asked his father. None of this made any sense to him.

Phil shrugged. "I don't know Nicole, but I don't like what I've heard. Be careful son. You don't want to lose what's most important over nothing. Use your common sense."

"I didn't seek her out, if that's what you're thinking," Cal said angrily.

"Did I say you had?"

This entire situation was out of control. If he'd known that recommending Nicole for a job at the bookstore would lead to this, he wouldn't have said a word. It didn't help any that Jane's best friend, Annie Porter, owned Tumbleweed Books, although he assumed Annie would show some discretion. He could trust her to believe him—but even if she didn't, Annie would never say or do anything to hurt Jane.

"You plan on seeing Nicole again?"

"I didn't plan on seeing her the first time," Cal shot back. "I don't have any reason to see her."

"Good. Keep it that way."

Cal didn't need his father telling him something

so obvious. Not until he reached the car did he remember the casserole dish. With his father's warning still ringing in his ears, he decided that returning it to Nicole could wait. When he had a chance, he'd tuck the glass dish in his pickup and drop it off at the bookstore. Besides, he no longer had the time. Because of this latest delay with his father, he'd have to hurry if he wanted to get to the airport before five, what with the rush hour traffic.

His wife and family were coming home.

Exhausted, Jane stepped off the plane, balancing Mary Ann on her hip. The baby had fussed the entire flight, and Jane suspected she might have an ear infection. Her skin was flushed and she was running a fever and tugging persistently at her ear.

With Mary Ann crying throughout most of the flight, Paul hadn't taken his nap and whined for the last hour, wanting to know when he could see his daddy again. Jane's own nerves were at the breaking point and she pitied her fellow passengers, although fortunately the plane had been half-empty.

''Where's Daddy?'' Paul said as they exited the jetway.

''He'll be here,'' Jane assured her son. The diaper bag slipped off her shoulder and tangled with her purse strap, weighing down her arm.

"I don't see Daddy," Paul cried, more loudly this time.

"He's here..." Jane said, straining to see through the crowd.

Only, Cal wasn't there. "He must've been held up in traffic," Jane muttered, struggling to hide her disappointment.

"You said Daddy would be here."

"I'm sure he's on his way," Jane told him, reaching for his hand. "Let's sit down here and wait a few minutes," she suggested, finding two seats together.

"I don't want to sit again," Paul complained. He crossed his arms defiantly. "I'm *tired* of sitting. I want my daddy."

"Fine. If you don't want to sit down, then stand by Mommy."

"No."

"Paul, please, I need you to be my helper."

Mary Ann started to cry, tugging at her ear. Jane did what she could to comfort her daughter, but it was clear the child was in pain. She had Children's Tylenol with her, but it was packed in the luggage. The checked luggage, of course.

Ten minutes later, after all the passengers had dispersed, Cal was still nowhere in sight. Jane glanced around, unsure what to do. Her husband had missed her so much he couldn't be bothered to get here on time to meet her flight?

In an attempt to remain calm, she decided to head toward the baggage area. If Cal did show up, he'd figure out where she was. If she got their suitcases, she could at least take out the medication for Mary Ann.

With the help of a friendly porter, she collected the suitcases and opened the smaller one, looking for the Tylenol. She'd found it just as she heard her name announced over the broadcast system.

''That must be your father,'' she told Paul.

''I want my daddy!'' the boy shrieked again.

Jane wanted Cal, too—and when she saw him she intended to let him know she was not pleased. She located a house phone, dragged over her bags and, kids in tow, breathlessly picked up the receiver.

She was put through to Cal.

''Where the hell are you?'' he snapped.

''Where the hell are *you?*'' She was tempted to remind him that she had three suitcases and two children to worry about, plus assorted other bags. The only items he had to carry were his wallet and car keys. Dammit all, she'd appreciate a little help!

''I went to the gate and saw that I'd missed you

and now I'm here in the baggage area," he told her a little more calmly.

"So am I."

"You aren't at carousel A."

"No, I'm one down at B. That's where I'm supposed to be." She tried to restrain her impatience. "Do you mind if we don't argue about this just now?"

"Stay right there and I'll meet you," Cal promised, sounding anxious.

Two minutes later Paul gave a loud cry. "Daddy! Daddy!"

There he was. Cal strolled toward them, wearing a wide grin as Paul raced in his direction. He looked wonderful, Jane had to admit. Tanned and relaxed, tall and lean. At the moment all she felt was exhausted. He reached down and scooped Paul into his arms, lifting him high. The boy wrapped his arms around Cal's neck and hugged him as though he never intended to let go.

"Welcome home," Cal said. Still holding Paul, he pulled her and the baby into his arms and gently embraced them.

"What happened?" Jane asked. "Where were you?"

"Kiss me first," he said, lowering his head to hers. The kiss was long and potent, and it told Jane in no uncertain terms how thrilled he was to have her back.

"I'm so glad to be home," she whispered.

"I'm damn glad you are, too." He placed his son back on the floor; Paul gripped his hand tightly. "I'm sorry about the mixup." Cal shook his head. "I gave myself plenty of time, but I stopped off to see my dad and got a later start than I wanted. And then traffic was bad."

Jane sighed. Of all the days to visit Phil! Knowing she was going to have her hands full, he might have been a bit more thoughtful.

The hour and a half ride into Promise didn't go smoothly, either. Keyed up and refusing to sleep, Paul was on his worst behavior. Mary Ann's medication took almost an hour to kick in, and until then, she cried and whimpered incessantly. Jane's nerves were stretched to the limit. Cal tried to distract both children with his own renditions of country classics, but he had little success.

When he pulled into the driveway, Jane gazed at the house with a sense of homecoming that nearly brought tears to her eyes. It'd been an emotional day from the first. Her mother had broken down when she dropped Jane and the kids off at LAX; seeing their grandmother weep, both children had started to cry, too. Then the flight and Mary Ann's fever and her difficulties at the airport. Instead of the loving reunion she'd longed for with Cal, there'd been one more disappointment.

"You and the kids go on inside, and I'll get the luggage," Cal told her.

"All right." Jane unfastened her now-sleeping daughter from the car seat and placed her against one shoulder.

Paul followed. "How come Daddy's going to his truck?" he asked.

Jane glanced over her shoulder. "I don't know." He seemed to be carrying something, but she couldn't see what and, frankly, she didn't care.

What Jane expected when she walked into the house was the same sense of welcome and familiar comfort. Instead, she walked into the kitchen—and found chaos. Dishes were stacked in the sink and three weeks' worth of mail was piled on the kitchen table. The garbage can was overflowing. Jane groaned and headed down the hallway. Dirty clothes littered the floor in front of the washer and dryer.

Attempting to take a positive view of the situation, Jane guessed this proved how much Cal needed her, how much she'd been missed.

She managed to keep her cool until she reached their bedroom. The bed was torn apart, the bedspread and blankets scattered across the floor, and that was her undoing. She proceeded to their daughter's room and gently set Mary Ann in her crib; fortunately she didn't wake up. Jane returned to the kitchen and met Cal just as he was walking in the back door with the last of her bags.

Hands on her hips, she glared at him. "You couldn't make the bed?"

"Ah..." He looked a bit sheepish. "I thought you'd want clean sheets."

"I do, but after three hours on a plane dealing with the kids, I didn't want to have to change them myself."

"Mommy! I'm hungry."

Jane had completely forgotten about dinner.

"The house is, uh, kind of a mess, isn't it?" Cal said guiltily. "I'm sorry, honey, my standards aren't as high as yours."

Rather than get involved in an argument, Jane went to the linen closet for a clean set of sheets. "Could you fix Paul a sandwich?" she asked.

"Sure," Cal said.

"I want tuna fish and pickles," Paul said.

"I suppose your mother let him eat any time he wanted," Cal grumbled.

Stephanie had, but that was beside the point. "Let's not get into this now," she said.

''All right.''

By the time Jane finished unpacking, sorting through the mail and separating laundry, it was nearly midnight. Cal helped her make the bed. He glanced repeatedly in her direction, looking apologetic.

''I'm sorry, honey,'' he said again.

Jane didn't want to argue, but this homecoming had fallen far short of what she'd hoped. At least Mary Ann was sleeping soundly. But without a nap, Paul had been completely out of sorts. Cal had put him down and returned a few minutes later complaining that his son had turned into a spoiled brat.

Jane had had enough. ''Don't even start,'' she warned him.

He held up both hands. ''All right, all right.''

They barely spoke afterward.

At last Cal undressed and slipped between the fresh sheets. ''You ready for bed?''

Exhausted, Jane merely nodded; she didn't have the energy to speak.

He held out his arms, urging her to join him, and one look told her what he had in mind.

Jane hesitated. ''I hope you're not thinking what I suspect you're thinking.''

''Honey,'' he pleaded, ''it's been nearly three weeks since we made love.''

Jane sagged onto the side of the bed. "Not tonight."

Cal looked crestfallen. "Okay, I guess I asked for that. You're upset about the house being a mess, aren't you?"

"I'm not punishing you, if that's what you're saying." Couldn't he see she was nearly asleep on her feet?

"Sure, whatever," he muttered. Jerking the covers past his shoulder, he rolled over and presented her with a view of his back.

"Oh, Cal, stop it," she said, wanting to shake him. He was acting like a spoiled little boy—like their own son when he didn't get what he wanted. At this point, though, Jane didn't care. She undressed and turned off the light. Tired as she was, she assumed she'd be asleep the instant her head hit the pillow.

She wasn't.

Instead, she lay awake in the dark, wondering how their reunion could possibly have gone so wrong.

Chapter 5

To say that Jane's kitchen cupboards were bare would be an understatement. One of her first chores the next morning was to buy groceries. Cal kept Paul with him for the day, instead of taking him to town for the church-run preschool, and Jane buckled Mary Ann into her car seat and drove to town.

She was grateful to be home, grateful to wake up with her husband at her side and grateful that the unpleasantness of the night before seemed to be forgotten. With the washer and dryer humming and the children well rested, the day looked brighter all around. Even Mary Ann seemed to be feeling better, and a quick check of her ears revealed no infection.

Although she had a whole list of things to do, Jane took time to stop by and see Ellie. Later, when she'd finished with her errands, she planned to make a quick run over to Annie's.

"You look..." Ellie hesitated as she met Jane outside Frasier Feed.

"Exhausted," Jane filled in for her. "I'm telling you, Ellie, this time away was no vacation."

"I know," Ellie said, steering her toward the old-fashioned rockers positioned in front. "I remember what it was like. With my dad sick and my mother frantic, it was all I could do to keep myself sane."

Jane wished Cal understood how trying and difficult these weeks had been for her. He *should* know, seeing that his own mother had been so terribly ill, but then, Phil had protected his sons from the truth for far too long.

"I'm glad you're home." Ellie sank into one of the rockers.

"Me, too." Jane sat down beside her friend, balancing Mary Ann on her knee. She loved sitting right here with Ellie, looking out at the town park and at the street; she'd missed their chats. She could smell mesquite smoke from the Chili Pepper. California cuisine had nothing on good old Texas barbecue, she thought, her mouth watering at the thought of ribs dripping with tangy sauce. A bowl of Nell's famous chili wouldn't go amiss, either.

"Everything will be better now," Ellie said.

Jane stared at her friend. "Better? How do you mean?"

Ellie's gaze instantly shot elsewhere. "It's nothing... I was thinking out loud. I'm just pleased you're back."

Jane was a little puzzled but let Ellie's odd remark slide. They talked about friends and family and planned a lunch date, then Jane left to get her groceries.

Buy-Right Foods had built a new supermarket on the outskirts of town, and it boasted one of the finest produce and seafood selections in the area. The day it opened, everyone in the county had shown up for the big event—and the music, the clowns who painted kids' faces and, not least, the generous assortment of free samples. There hadn't been a parking space in the lot, which had occasioned plenty of complaints. People didn't understand that this kind of congestion was a way of life in California. Jane had forgotten what it was like to wait through two cycles at a traffic light just to reach a left-turn lane. A traffic jam in Promise usually meant two cars at a stop sign.

Grabbing a cart at the Buy-Right, she fastened Mary Ann into the seat and headed down the first aisle. Everyone who saw Jane seemed to stop and chat, welcome her home. At this rate, it'd take all day to gather the items on her list. Actually she didn't mind. If Cal had shown half the enthusiasm her friends and neighbors did, the unpleasantness the night before might have been averted.

"Jane Dickinson—I mean, Patterson! Why, I do declare you're a sight for sore eyes."

Jane recognized the voice immediately. Tammy Lee Kollenborn. The woman was a known flirt and troublemaker. Jane tended to avoid her, remembering the grief Tammy had caused Dovie several years earlier. After a ten-year relationship, Dovie had wanted to get married and Frank hadn't. Then, for some ridiculous reason, Frank had asked Tammy Lee out. The night had been a disaster, and shortly afterward Frank had proposed to Dovie— although not before Tammy had managed to upset Dovie with her lies and insinuations.

"Hello, Tammy Lee."

Her gold heels made flip-flop sounds as the older woman pushed her cart alongside Jane's. "My, your little one sure is a cutie-pie." She peered at Mary Ann through her rhinestone-rimmed glasses.

"I swear I'd die for lashes that long," she said, winking up at Jane.

Trying to guess Tammy Lee's age was a fruitless effort. She dressed in a style Jane privately called "Texas trash" and wore enough costume jewelry to qualify her for a weight-lifting award.

"From what I understand, it's a good thing you got home when you did," Tammy Lee said in a low voice.

Jane frowned. "Why?"

Tammy Lee glanced over her shoulder. "You mean to say no one's mentioned what's been going on with Cal and that other woman while you were away?"

Jane pinched her lips. If she was smart, she'd make a convenient excuse and leave without giving Tammy the pleasure of spreading her lies. They *had* to be lies. After five years of marriage, Jane knew her husband, and Cal was not the type of man to cheat on his wife.

"Her name's Nicole Nelson. Pretty thing. Younger than you by a good, oh, six or seven years, although it's hard to say for sure. Bearing children ages a woman, you know. My first husband wanted kids, but I knew the minute I got pregnant I'd eat my way through the entire pregnancy. So I refused.''

''Yes, well…listen, Tammy Lee, I've got a million things to do.''

''I saw Cal with her myself.''

''I really do need to be going—''

''They were having dinner together at the Mexican Lindo.''

''Cal and Nicole Nelson?'' Jane refused to believe it.

''They were *whispering*. This is a small town, Jane, and people notice these things. Like I said, I'm surprised no one's mentioned it. I probably shouldn't, either, but my fourth husband cheated on me and I would've given anything for someone to tell me sooner. You've heard the saying? The wife is always the last to know.''

''I'm sure there's a very logical reason Cal was with Nicole,'' Jane insisted, not allowing herself to feel jealous. Even if she was, she wouldn't have said anything in front of Tammy Lee.

''Isn't that something?'' Tammy Lee said, laughing lightly. ''When my dear friend finally broke down and told me about Mark seeing another woman, I said the very same thing. Wives are simply too trusting. We naturally assume our husbands would never betray us like that.''

''I really have a lot to do,'' Jane said again.

''Now, you listen to me, Jane. I want you to remember later on, when you're forced to deal with this betrayal, that I'm here for you. I know what you're feeling.''

Jane was sure that couldn't be true.

''If you need someone to talk to, come to me. I've been down this road myself. If you need a good attorney, I can recommend one in San Antonio. When she's finished with Cal Patterson, he won't have a dime.''

''Tammy Lee, I don't have time for this,'' Jane said, and forcefully pushed her cart forward.

''Call me, you hear?'' Tammy Lee gently patted Jane's shoulder. Jane found it a patronizing gesture and had to grit her teeth.

By the time she'd finished paying for the groceries, she was furious. No one needed to tell her who Nicole Nelson was; Jane remembered the other woman all too well. Nicole had sought Cal out the afternoon of the rodeo. Jane had sat in the grandstand with her two children while that woman flirted outrageously with her husband.

For now, Jane was willing to give Cal the benefit

of the doubt. But as she loaded the groceries into the car, she remembered Ellie's strange comment about everything being "better" now. So *that* was what her sister-in-law had meant.

The one person she trusted to talk this out with was Dovie. Jane hurried to her friend's antique store, although she couldn't stay long.

Dovie greeted her with a hug. The store looked wonderful, thanks to Dovie's gift for display. Her assortment of antiques, jewelry, dried flowers, silk scarves and more was presented in appealing and imaginative ways.

They chatted a few minutes while Dovie inquired about Jane's parents.

"I ran into Tammy Lee Kollenborn at Buy-Right Foods," Jane announced suddenly, watching Dovie's reaction. It didn't take long for her to see one. "So it's true?"

"Now, Jane—"

"Cal's been seeing Nicole Nelson?"

"I wouldn't say that."

"According to Tammy Lee, they were together at the Mexican Lindo. Is that right?"

Hands clenched in front of her, Dovie hesitated, then nodded.

Jane couldn't believe her ears. She felt as though her legs were about to collapse out from under her.

"I'm sure there's a perfectly logical reason," Dovie said weakly, and Jane realized she'd said the very same words herself not ten minutes earlier.

"If that's the case, then why didn't Cal mention it?" she demanded, although she didn't expect an answer from Dovie.

The older woman's gaze shifted uncomfortably. "You'll have to ask him."

"Oh, I intend to," Jane muttered as she headed out the door. She'd visit Annie another day. Right now, she was more interested in hearing what Cal had to say for himself.

When she pulled off the highway and hurtled down the long drive to the ranch house, the first thing she noticed was that the screen door was open. Cal and Paul walked out to the back porch to greet her. She saw that her husband's expression was slightly embarrassed, as if he knew he'd done something wrong.

"Don't be mad," he said when she stepped out of the car, "but Paul and I had a small accident."

"What kind of accident?" she asked.

"We decided to make lunch for you and...well, let me just say that I think we can save the pan."

A smile started to quiver at the corners of his mouth. "Come on, honey, it's only a pan. I'm sure the smoke will wash off the walls."

"Tell me about Nicole Nelson," Jane said, point-blank.

The amusement vanished from his eyes. He stiffened. "What's there to say?"

"Plenty, from what I hear."

"Come on, Jane, you know me better than that."

"Do I?" She glared at him.

"Jane, you're being ridiculous."

"Did you or did you not have dinner with Nicole Nelson?"

Cal didn't answer.

"It's a simple question," she said, growing impatient.

"Yeah, but the answer is complicated."

"I damn well bet it is!" Jane was angrier than she could remember being in a very long while. If they'd had a wonderful reunion, she might have found the whole matter forgettable. Instead, he hadn't bothered to show up at the airport until after she'd landed. The house was a mess and all he could think about was getting her in the sack. She shifted Mary Ann on her hip, grabbed a plastic bag full of groceries and stomped into the house.

"Jane!"

She stood in the doorway. "I have all the answers I need."

"Fine!" Cal shouted, angry now.

"Daddy, Daddy!" Paul cried, covering his ears. "Mommy's mad."

"Is this what you want out son to see?" Cal yelled after her.

"That's just perfect," Jane yelled back. "You're running around town with another woman, you don't offer a word of explanation and then you blame *me* because our son sees us fighting." Hurt, angry and outraged, she stormed into the bedroom.

No one needed to tell Glen that things weren't going well between his brother and Jane. He saw evidence of the trouble in their marriage every morning when he drove to work at the Lonesome Coyote Ranch.

He and Cal were partners, had worked together for years, and if anyone knew that Cal could be unreasonable, it was Glen. More important, though, Glen was well aware that his older brother loved his wife and children.

By late October the demands of raising cattle had peaked for the season, since most of their herd had been sold off. Not that the hours Cal kept gave any indication of that. Most mornings when Glen arrived, Cal had already left the house.

"Are you going to talk about it?" Glen asked him late one afternoon. Cal hadn't said more than two words to him all day. They sat side by side in the truck, driving back to the ranch house.

"No," Cal barked.

"This has to do with Jane, right?" Glen asked.

Cal purposely hit a pothole, which made Glen bounce so high in his seat that his head hit the truck roof, squashing the crown of his Stetson.

"Dammit, Cal, there was no call for that," Glen muttered, repairing his hat.

"Sorry," Cal returned, but his tone said he was anything but.

"If you can't talk to me, then who can you talk to?" Glen asked. It bothered him that his only brother refused to even acknowledge, let alone discuss, his problems. Over the years Glen had spilled his guts any number of times. More than once Cal had steered him away from trouble. Glen was ready to do him the same favor.

"If I *wanted* to talk, you mean," Cal said.

"In other words, you'd prefer to keep it all to yourself."

"Yup."

"Fine, then, if that's what you want."

They drove several minutes in tense silence. Finally Glen couldn't stand it any longer. "This is your wife—your *family*. Doesn't that matter to you? What's going on?" He could feel his patience with Cal fading."

Cal grumbled something he couldn't hear. Then he said in a grudging voice, "Jane paid a visit to Tumbleweed Books the other day."

His brother didn't need to explain further. Nicole Nelson worked at the bookstore, and although Jane was good friends with Annie Porter, Glen suspected she hadn't casually dropped by to see her.

"She talk to Nicole?"

Cal shrugged. "I don't like my wife checking up on me."

Glen mulled this over and wondered if Cal had explained the situation. "Jane knows you didn't take Nicole to dinner, doesn't she?"

"Yes, dammit!" he shouted. "I told her what happened. The next thing I know, she's all bent out of shape, slamming pots and pans around the kitchen like I did something terrible."

"Make it up to her," Glen advised. If his brother

hadn't learned that lesson by now, it was high time he did.

"I didn't do anything," Cal snapped. "If she doesn't believe me, then..." He let the rest fade.

"Cal, get real! Do what you've got to do, man. You aren't the only one, you know. Ellie gets a bee in her bonnet every now and then. Hell if I know what I did wrong, but after a while I don't care. I want things settled. I want peace in the valley. Learn from me—apologize and be done with it."

Cal frowned, shaking his head. "I'm not you."

"Pride can make a man damned miserable," Glen said. "It's...it's like sitting on a barbed-wire fence naked." He nodded, pleased with his analogy.

Cal shook his head again, and Glen doubted his brother had really heard him. Deciding to change the subject, Glen tried another approach. "How's Jane's father?"

"All right, I guess. She talks to her mother damn near every day."

The ranch house came into view. Glen recalled a time not so long ago when they'd reached this same spot and had seen Nicole Nelson's vehicle parked down below. A thought occurred to him, a rather unpleasant one.

"Are you still in love with Jane?" Glen asked.

Cal hit the brakes with enough force to throw them both forward. If not for the restraint of the seat belts, they might have hit their heads on the windshield.

"What the hell kind of question is that?" Cal roared.

"Do you still love Jane?" Glen yelled right back.

"Of course I do!"

Glen relaxed.

"What I want is a wife who trusts me," Cal said. "I haven't so much as looked at another woman since the day we met, and she damn well knows it."

"Maybe she doesn't."

"Well, she should," was his brother's response.

To Glen's way of thinking, there were plenty of things a wife should know and often didn't. He figured it was the man's job to set things straight and to make sure that his wife was left without any doubt about his feelings.

In the days that followed it was clear that the situation between Jane and Cal hadn't improved. Feeling helpless, Glen decided to seek his father's advice. He found Phil at the bowling alley Friday afternoon, when the senior league was just finishing up. It didn't take much to talk Phil into coffee and a piece of pecan pie. The bowling alley café still served the best breakfast in town and was a popular place to eat.

As soon as they slid into the booth, the waitress automatically brought over the coffeepot.

"We'll each have a slice of pecan pie, Denise," Phil told her.

"Coming right up," she said, filling the thick white mugs with an expert hand. "How you doin', Phil? Glen?"

"Good," Glen answered for both of them.

No more than a minute later they were both served generous slices of pie. "Enjoy," she said cheerily."

Phil reached for his fork. "No problem there."

Glen wasn't as quick to grab his own fork. He had a lot on his mind.

"You want to talk to me about something?" Phil asked, busy doctoring his coffee.

Glen left his black and raised the mug, sipping carefully.

"I didn't figure you were willing to buy me a slice of pecan pie for nothing."

Glen chuckled. Of the two sons, he shared his father's temperament. Their mother had been a take-charge kind of woman and Cal got that from her, but she'd never held her hurts close to the chest, like Cal did.

"I take it you're worried about your brother." Phil picked up his fork again and cut into his pie.

"Yeah." Glen stared down at his favorite dessert and realized he didn't have much of an appetite. "What can I say to him?"

"Listen." Phil leaned forward to rest his elbows on the table. "When your mother was alive and we had the bed-and-breakfast, she was constantly try-ing new recipes."

Glen couldn't understand what his mother's cooking had to do with the current situation, but he knew better than to ask. Phil would get around to explaining sooner or later.

"No matter what time of day it was, she'd sit down and dish up a serving. When I asked her why, she said it was important to try a little of it herself before she served it to anyone else."

"Okay," Glen said, still wondering what the connection was between his mother's culinary ex-periments and Cal and Jane.

"Advice is like that. Take some yourself before you hand it to others."

"I haven't given Cal any advice." Not for lack

of trying, however. Cal simply wasn't in the mood to listen to it.

"I realize that. The advice is going to come from me, and I'm giving it to you—free of charge."

Glen laughed, shaking his head.

"Let Cal and Jane settle this matter themselves."

"But, Dad..."

Phil waved his fork at him. "Every couple has problems at one time or another. You and Ellie will probably go through a difficult patch yourselves, and when you do, you won't appreciate other people sticking their noses in your business."

"Do you think Cal and Jane are going to be okay?"

"Of course they are. Cal loves Jane. He isn't going to do anything to jeopardize his family. Now eat your pie, or I just might find an excuse to help myself to a second slice."

Glen picked up his fork. His father knew what he was talking about; Cal did love Jane, and whatever was wrong would eventually right itself.

Jane noticed a change in Cal the moment he came into the house. They'd been ignoring each other all week. The tension was taking its toll, not only on her but on the children.

Her husband paused in the middle of the kitchen, where she was busy putting together Halloween costumes for the children. As usual the church was holding a combined harvest and Halloween party.

Jane didn't leave her place at the kitchen table, nor did she speak to Cal. Instead, she waited for him to make the first move, which he did. He walked over to the stove and poured himself a cup of coffee, then approached the table.

"What are you doing?" he asked in a friendly voice.

"Making Mary Ann a costume for the church party." She gestured at a piece of white fabric printed with spots. "She's going as a dalmatian," Jane said.

Cal grinned. "One of the hundred and one?"

Jane nodded and held up a black plastic dog nose, complete with elastic tie.

"What about Paul?"

"He's going as a pirate."

Cal cradled his mug in both hands. "Do you mind if I sit down?"

"Please."

He pulled out the chair and set his coffee on the table. For at least a minute, he didn't say a word. When he finally spoke, his voice was low, deliberate. "This whole thing about Nicole Nelson is totally out of control. If you need reassurances, then I'll give them to you. I swear to you not a damn thing happened."

Jane said nothing. It'd taken him nearly two weeks to tell her what she already knew. His unwillingness to do so earlier had hurt her deeply. In her heart she knew she could trust her husband, but his pride and stubbornness had shut her out.

This situation with Nicole was unfortunate. Not wanting to put Annie in the middle—it was awkward with Nicole working at Tumbleweed Books— Jane had asked general questions about the other woman. Annie had assured her that she liked Nicole. After their talk, Jane was convinced that the encounter between Nicole and Cal, whatever it was, had been completely innocent.

Because they lived in a small town, the story had spread quickly and the truth had gotten stretched out of all proportion; Jane understood that. What troubled her most was Cal's attitude. Instead of answering her questions or reiterating his love, he'd acted as if *she'd* been the one to wrong him. Well, *she* hadn't been out there generating gossip! Still, she felt a sense of relief that their quarrel was ending.

Jane found her husband staring at her intently.

"Can we put this behind us?" Cal asked.

Jane smiled. "I think it's time, don't you?"

Cal's shoulders relaxed, and he nodded. The next thing Jane knew, she was in her husband's arms and he was kissing her with familiar passion. "I'm crazy about you, Jane," he whispered, weaving his fingers into the thick locks of her hair.

"I don't like it when we fight," she confessed, clinging to him.

"You think I do?" he asked. "Especially over something as stupid as this."

"Oh, Cal," she breathed as he bent to kiss her again.

"Want to put the kids to bed early tonight?"

She nodded eagerly and brought her mouth to his. "Right after dinner."

Afterward, Jane felt worlds better about everything. They'd both been at fault to let the situation drag on, and they both swore it wouldn't happen again.

For the next few days Cal was loving and attentive, and so was Jane, but it didn't take them long to slip back into the old patterns. The first time she became aware of it was the night of the church harvest party.

Amy McMillen, the pastor's wife, had asked Jane to arrive early to assist her in setting up for the big do. She'd assumed Cal would be driving her into town. Instead, he announced that he intended to stay home and catch up on paperwork. Jane made sure Cal knew she wanted him to attend the function with her, that she needed his help. Managing both children, plus assisting with one of the games, would be virtually impossible otherwise. But she decided not to complain; she'd done so much of that in the past couple of months.

When it came time for her to leave, Cal walked her and the children out to the car. Once she'd buckled the kids into their seats, she started the engine, but Cal stopped her.

"You've got a headlight out."

"I do? Oh, no..."

"I don't want you driving into town with only one headlight."

Jane glanced at her watch.

"Take the truck," he advised. "I'll change the car seats."

"But—"

"Sweetheart, please, it'll just take a minute." Fortunately his truck was a large four-door variety with ample space for both seats.

"What's this?" Jane asked. In front, on the passenger side was a cardboard box with a glass casserole dish.

Cal took one look at it and his eyes rushed to meet hers. "A dish," he muttered.

"Of course it's a dish. *Whose* dish?"

He shrugged as if it was no big deal. "I don't know if I mentioned it, but Dovie and Savannah brought me meals while you were away," he said, wrapping the safety belt around Mary Ann's car seat and snapping it into place.

"You mean to say half the town was feeding you and you still managed to nearly destroy my kitchen?"

Cal chuckled.

"I meant to return the dish long before now." He kissed Jane and closed the passenger door. "I'll see to that headlight first thing tomorrow morning," he promised, and opened the door on the driver's side.

Jane climbed in behind the wheel. Normally she didn't like driving Cal's vehicle, which was high off the ground and had a stick shift. She agreed, however, that in the interests of safety, it was the better choice.

The church was aglow when Jane drove up. Pastor Wade McMillen stood outside, welcoming early arrivals, and when he saw Jane, he walked over and helped her extract Mary Ann from her car seat.

"Glad to have you back, Jane," he said. "I hope everything went well with your father."

"He's doing fine," she said, although that wasn't entirely true. She was in daily communication with her mother. It seemed her father wasn't responding to the chemotherapy anymore and grew weaker with every treatment. Her mother was at a loss. Several times she'd broken into tears, and asked Jane to talk Cal into letting her and the children come back for a visit over Christmas. Knowing how Cal would react, she hadn't broached the subject yet.

"Would you like me to carry in that box for you?" Wade asked.

"Please." What a good idea. Both Dovie and Savannah would be at the church party, and there was no reason to keep that casserole dish in the truck.

"I'll put it in the kitchen," Wade told her, leading the way.

Paul saw the display of pumpkins and dried cornstalks in the large meeting room and gave a shout of sheer delight. Although it was early, the place was hopping, and children ran in every direction.

Jane followed the pastor into the kitchen, and sure enough, found Dovie there.

''I understand this is yours,'' Jane said when Wade set the box down on the countertop.

Dovie shook her head.

''Didn't you send dinner out to Cal?''

''I did, but he already returned the dishes.''

''It must belong to Savannah, then,'' she said absently.

Not until much later in the evening did Jane see Savannah and learn otherwise. ''Well, for heaven's sake,'' she muttered to Ellie as they were busy with the cleanup. ''I don't want to drag this dish back home. Do you know who it belongs to?''

Ellie went suspiciously quiet.

''Ellie?'' Jane asked, not understanding at first.

''Ask Cal,'' her sister-in-law suggested.

''Cal?'' Jane repeated and then it hit her—like a lightning bolt. She knew *exactly* who owned that casserole dish. And asking Cal was what she intended to do. Clearly more had gone on while she was away than he'd admitted. How dared he do this to her!

Glen carried the box containing the dish back to

the truck for her. Tired from the party, both Paul and Mary Ann fell asleep long before she turned off the highway onto the dirt road that led to the house.

No sooner had she parked the truck than the back door opened and Cal stepped out. Although it was difficult to contain herself, she waited until both children were in bed before she brought up the subject of the unclaimed dish.

"I ran into Dovie and Savannah," she said casually as they walked into the living room, where the television was on. Apparently her husband didn't have as much paperwork as he'd suggested.

"Oh? How was the party?"

Jane ignored the question. "Neither one of them owns that casserole dish."

Jane watched as Cal's shoulders tensed.

"Tell me, Cal Patterson, who does own it?"

Cal strode to the far side of the room, putting the entire length of the room between them.

"Don't tell me you've forgotten," Jane said.

He shook his head.

A sick feeling was beginning to build in the pit of her stomach. "Cal?"

"Sweetheart, listen—"

"All I want is a name," she interrupted, folding

her arms and letting her actions tell him she was in no mood to be cajoled.

Cal started to say something, then stopped.

''You don't need to worry,'' Jane said without emotion. ''I figured it out. That dish belongs to Nicole Nelson.''

Chapter 6

Cal couldn't believe this was happening. Okay, so his wife had reason to be upset. He probably should've mentioned that Nicole Nelson had brought him a meal. The only reason he hadn't was that he was hoping to avoid yet another argument. He knew how much their disagreements distressed her, and she'd been through so much lately. He'd just been trying to protect her!

Without a word to him, Jane had gone to bed. Cal gave her a few minutes to cool down before he ventured into the bedroom. The lights were off, but he knew she wasn't asleep.

"Honey," he said, and sat on the edge of the bed. Jane had her back to him and was so far over on her side of the bed it was a wonder she hadn't tumbled out. "Can we talk about this?" he asked, willing to take his punishment, and be done with it.

"No."

"You're right, I should've told you Nicole came to the ranch, but I swear she wasn't here more than fifteen minutes. If that. She dropped off the casserole and that was it."

Jane flopped over onto her back. "Are you sure, or is there something else you're conveniently forgetting to mention?"

Cal could live without the sarcasm, but let it drop. "I thought we'd decided to put this behind us." He could always hope tonight's installment of their ongoing argument would be quickly settled. The constant tension between them had worn his patience thin.

Jane suddenly bolted upright in bed. She reached for the lamp beside her bed and flipped the switch, casting a warm light about the room. "You have a very bad habit of keeping things from me."

That was unfair! Cal thought. He took a deep calming breath before responding. "It's true I didn't tell you Nicole fixed me dinner, but—"

"You didn't so much as mention her name!"

"Okay...but when was I supposed to do that? You were in California, remember?"

"We talked on the phone nearly every night," Jane said, crossing her arms. "Now that I think about it, you kept the conversations short and sweet, didn't you? Was there a reason for that?''

Again, Cal resented the implication, but again he swallowed his annoyance and said, ''You know I'm not much of a conversationalist.'' Chatting on the phone had always felt awkward to him. Jane knew that.

''What else haven't you told me about you and Nicole Nelson? How many other times have you two met without my knowing? When she brought you dinner, did she make a point of joining you? Did you accidentally bump into each other in town a couple of times?''

''No,'' he answered from between gritted teeth.

''You're sure?''

''Dammit, Jane, you make it sound like I'm having an affair with her! I've done nothing wrong, not a damn thing!''

''Tell me why I should believe you, seeing how you habitually conceal things from me.''

''You think I purposely hid the truth?'' Their marriage was in sad shape if she made such assumptions. Jane was his partner in life; he'd shared every aspect of his business, his home and his ranch with her, fathered two children with her. It came as a shock that she didn't trust him.

"What about the rodeo?" she asked. "You signed up for the bull-riding competition and you deliberately didn't mention it to me."

"I knew you didn't want me participating in the rodeo, and—"

"What I don't know won't hurt me, right?"

She had a way of twisting his words into knots no cowhand could untangle, himself included. "All right, all right, you win. I'm a rotten husband. That's what you want to hear, isn't it?"

Her eyes flared and she shook her head. "What I want to hear is the truth."

"I tell you the truth!" he shouted, losing his temper.

"But not until you're backed into a corner."

"I've been as honest with you as I know how." Cal tried again, but he'd reached his limit. Glen had advised him to say what he had to say, do what he had to do—whatever it took to make up with Jane. He'd attempted that once already, but it hadn't been enough. Not only was she not satisfied, now she was looking to collect a piece of his soul right along with that pound of flesh.

"Why didn't you attend the church party with me and the kids?" she asked.

He frowned. Jane knew the answer to that as well

as he did. "I already told you. I had paperwork to do."

"How long did it take you?"

Cal ran a hand down his face. "Is there a reason you're asking?"

"A very good one," she informed him coolly. "I'm trying to find out if you slipped away to be with Nicole."

If his wife had pulled out a gun and shot him, Cal couldn't have been more staggered. He jumped off the bed and stood there staring, dumbstruck that Jane would actually suggest such a thing.

"I noticed you had the television on," she continued. "So you finished with all that paperwork earlier than you anticipated. Did you stop to think about me coping with the children alone? All you wanted was a quiet evening at home while I was left to manage the children, the party and everything else on my own."

"For the love of God, would you listen to yourself?"

"I *am* listening," she shouted. "You sent me off to deal with my family, then you're seen around town with another woman. If *that* isn't enough, you lie and mislead me into thinking I'm overreacting. All at once everything's beginning to add up, and frankly I don't like the total. You're interested in having an affair with her, aren't you, Cal? That's what I see.''

Cal had no intention of commenting on anything so ludicrous.

''What's the matter? Am I too close to the truth?''

Shaking his head, Cal looked down at her, unable to hide his disgust. ''Until this moment I've never regretted marrying you.'' He headed out the door, letting it slam behind him.

Almost immediately the bedroom door flew open again. ''You think *I* don't have regrets about marrying *you?*'' Jane railed. ''You're not alone in that department, Cal Patterson.'' Once again the door was slammed with such force that he was sure he'd have to nail the molding back in place.

Not knowing where to go or what else to say, Cal stood in the middle of the darkened living room. In five years of marriage he and Jane had disagreed before, but never like this. He glanced toward their bedroom and knew there'd be hell to pay if he tried to sleep there.

Cal sat in his recliner, raised the footrest and covered himself with the afghan he'd grabbed from the back of the sofa.

Everything would be better in the morning, he told himself.

Cal had left the house by the time Jane awoke. It was what she'd expected. What she *wanted*, she told herself. Luckily the children had been asleep and hadn't heard them fighting. She got her robe from the back of the door and slipped it on. Sick at heart, she felt as though she hadn't slept all night.

The coffee was already made when she wandered into the kitchen. She was just pouring herself a cup when Paul appeared, dragging his favorite blanket.

''Where's Daddy?'' he asked, rubbing his eyes.

''He's with Uncle Glen.'' Jane crouched down to give her son a hug.

Paul pulled away and met her look, his dark eyes sad. ''Is Daddy mad at you?''

''No, darling, Daddy and Mommy love each other very much.'' She was certain Cal regretted the argument as much as she did. She reached for her son and hugged him again.

Their fight had solved nothing. They'd both said things that should never have been said. The sudden tears that rushed into Jane's eyes were unexpected, and she didn't immediately realize she was crying. The children *had* heard their argument. At least

Paul must have, otherwise he wouldn't be asking these questions.

"Mommy?" Paul touched his fingers to her face, saw her tears, then broke away from her and raced into the other room. He returned a moment later with a box of tissues, which made Jane weep all the more. How could her beautiful son be so thoughtful and sweet, and his father so insensitive, so unreasonable?

After making breakfast for Paul and Mary Ann and getting them dressed, Jane left the house to drive her son to preschool. The truck was parked where she'd left it the night before. Apparently Cal had gone out on Fury, his favorite gelding. He often rode when he needed time to think.

Peering into the truck, Jane saw that the casserole dish was still there. She looked at it for a moment, then removed it and placed it in the car. While Paul was in his preschool class, she'd return it personally to Nicole Nelson. And when she did, Jane planned to let her know how happily married Cal Patterson was.

After dropping Paul off, Jane drove to Tumbleweed Books.

"Hello," Nicole Nelson called out when Jane walked into the store. Jane recognized her right away. The only previous time she'd seen the other woman had been at the rodeo, and that was from a distance. On closer inspection, she had to admit that Nicole was a beautiful woman. Jane instantly felt dowdy and unkempt. She wished she'd taken more time with her hair and makeup, especially since she'd decided to meet Nicole face-to-face.

"Is there anything I can help you find?" Nicole asked, glancing at Mary Ann in her stroller.

"Is Annie available?" Jane asked, making a sudden decision that when she did confront Nicole, she'd do it when she looked her best.

"I'm sorry, Annie had a doctor's appointment this morning. I'd be delighted to assist you, if I can."

So polite and helpful. So insincere. Jane didn't even know Nicole Nelson, and already she disliked her.

"That's all right. I'll come back another time." Feeling foolish, Jane was eager to leave.

"I don't believe we've met," Nicole said. "I'm Annie's new sales assistant, Nicole Nelson."

Jane had no option but to introduce herself. She straightened and looked directly at Nicole. "I'm Jane Patterson."

"Cal's wife," Nicole said, not missing a beat. A

slow knowing smile appeared on her face as she boldly met Jane's eye.

Standing no more than two feet apart, Jane and Nicole stared hard at each other. In that moment Jane knew the awful truth. Nicole Nelson wanted her husband. Wanted him enough to destroy Jane and ruin her marriage. Wanted him enough to deny his children their father. Cal was a challenge to her, a prize to be won, no matter what the cost.

"I believe I have something of yours," Jane said.

Nicole's smile became a bit cocky. "I believe you do."

"Luckily I brought the casserole dish with me," Jane returned just as pointedly. She bent down, retrieved it from the stroller and handed it to Nicole.

"Did Cal happen to mention if he liked my taco casserole?" Nicole asked, following Jane to the front of the bookstore.

"Oh," Jane murmured, ever so sweetly, "he said it was much too spicy for him."

"I don't think so," Nicole said, holding open one of the doors. "I think Cal might just find he prefers a bit of spice compared to the bland taste he's used to."

Fuming, Jane pushed Mary Ann's stroller out the door and discovered, when she reached the car, that her hands were trembling. This was worse than she'd anticipated. Because now she had reason to wonder if her husband had fallen willingly into the other woman's schemes.

Jane had a knot in her stomach for the rest of the day. She was sliding a roast into the oven as Cal walked into the house shortly after four-thirty—early for him. He paused when he saw her, then lowered his head and walked past, ignoring her.

"I...think we should talk," she said, closing the oven, then leaning weakly against it. She set the pot holders aside and forced herself to straighten.

"Now?" Cal asked, as though any discussion with her was an unpleasant prospect.

"Paul...heard us last night," she said. She glanced into the other room, where their son was watching a Barney video. Mary Ann sat next to him, tugging at her shoes and socks.

"It's not surprising he heard us," Cal said evenly. "You nearly tore the door off the hinges when you slammed it."

Cal had slammed the door first, but now didn't seem to be the time to point that out. "He had his blankey this morning."

"I thought you threw that thing away," Cal said, making it sound like an accusation.

"He...found it. Obviously he felt he needed it."

Cal's eyes narrowed, and she knew he'd seen through her explanation.

"That isn't important. What *is* important, at least to me," she said, pressing her hand to her heart, "is that we not argue in front of the children."

"So you're saying we can go into the barn and shout at each other all we want? Should we call ahead and arrange for a baby-sitter first?"

Jane reached behind her to grab hold of the oven door. The day had been bad enough, and she wanted only to repair the damage that had been done to their relationship. This ongoing dissatisfaction with each other seemed to be getting worse; Jane knew it had to stop.

"I don't think I slept five minutes last night," she whispered.

Cal said nothing.

"I...I don't know what's going on between you and Nicole Nelson, but—"

Cal started to walk away from her.

"Cal!" she cried, stopping him.

"Nothing, Jane. There's nothing going on between me and Nicole Nelson. I don't know how many times I have to say it, and frankly, I'm getting tired of it."

Jane swallowed hard but tried to remain out-
wardly calm. "She wants you."

Cal's response was a short disbelieving laugh.
"That's crazy."

Jane shook her head. There'd been no mistaking
what she'd read in the other woman's expression.
Nicole had set her sights on Cal and was determined to do whatever she could to get him. Jane
had to give her credit. Nicole wasn't overtly trying
to seduce him. That would have gotten her nowhere
with Cal, and somehow she knew it. Instead, Nicole
had attacked the foundation of their marriage, cre-
ating doubt and mistrust between the two of them.
She must be pleased with her victory. At this point
Jane and Cal were barely talking.

"Just a minute," Cal said, frowning darkly.
"Did you purposely seek out Nicole? Again?"

Jane's shoulders heaved as she expelled a deep
sigh. "This is the first time I've met her."

"Where?"

"I went by the bookstore after I dropped Paul
off at preschool."

"To see Annie?"

"No," she admitted reluctantly. "I decided since
I was in town, I'd return the casserole dish."

Jane watched as Cal's gaze widened and his jaw went white with the effort to restrain his anger.

"That was wrong?" she blurted.

"Yes, dammit!"

"You wanted to bring it back yourself, is that it?"

He slapped the table so hard that the saltshaker toppled onto its side. "You went in search of Nicole Nelson. Did you ever stop to think that might embarrass me?"

Stunned, she felt her mouth open. "You're afraid I might have embarrassed *you?* That's rich." Despite herself, Jane's control began to slip. "How dare you say such a thing to me?" she cried. "What about everything you've done to embarrass *me?* I'm the one who's been humiliated here. While I'm away dealing with a family crisis, my husband's seen with another woman. And everyone's talking about it."

"I'd hoped you'd be above listening to malicious gossip."

"Oh, Cal, how can you say that? I was thrust right into the middle of it, and you know what? I didn't enjoy the experience."

He shook his head, still frowning. "You had no business confronting Nicole."

"No business?" she echoed, outraged. "How can you be so callous about my feelings? Don't you see what she's doing? Don't you understand? She wants you, Cal, and she didn't hide the fact, either. Are you going to let her destroy us? Are you?"

"This isn't about Nicole!" he shouted. "It's about trust and commitment."

"*Are* you committed to me?" she asked.

The look on his face answered her question. "If you have to ask, that says everything."

"It does, doesn't it?" Jane felt shaky, almost light-headed. "I never thought it'd come to this," she said, swallowing the pain. "Not with us..." She felt disillusioned and broken. Sinking into a chair, she buried her face in her hands.

"Jane." Cal stood on the other side of the table. She glanced up.

"Neither of us got much sleep last night."

"I don't think—"

The phone rang, and Cal sighed irritably as he walked over and snatched up the receiver. His voice sharp, he said, "Hello," and then he went still and his face instantly sobered. His gaze shot to her.

"She's here," he said. "Yes, yes, I understand."

Jane didn't know what to make of this. "Cal?" she said getting to her feet. The phone call seemed to be for her. As she approached, she heard her husband say that he'd tell her. *Tell her what?*

Slowly Cal replaced the receiver. He put his hands on her shoulders and his eyes searched hers. ''That was your uncle Ken,'' he said quietly and with obvious reluctance.

''Uncle Ken? Why didn't he talk to me?'' Jane demanded, and then intuition took over and she knew without asking. ''What's wrong with my dad?''

Cal looked away for a moment. ''Your father suffered a massive heart attack this afternoon.''

A chill raced through her, a chill of fear and foreboding. Instantly the numbness was replaced by a list of the cardiac specialists she knew in Southern California, doctors her family should contact. Surely her uncle Ken had already reached someone. He was an experienced physician; he'd know what to do, who to call.

''What did he say?''

''Jane—''

''You should've let me talk to him.''

''Jane.'' His hands gripped her shoulders as he tried to get her attention. ''It's too late. Your father's gone.''

She froze. Gone? Her father was dead? No! It

couldn't be true. Not her father, not her daddy. Her knees buckled and she was immediately over-whelmed by deep heart-wrenching sobs.

"Honey, I'm so sorry." Cal pulled her into his arms and held her as she sobbed.

Jane had never experienced pain at this level. She could barely think, barely function. First they thought they'd leave the children with Glen and El-lie; later Jane decided she wanted them with her. While Cal called the airlines and made flight ar-rangements, she packed suitcases for him and the kids. Only when Cal started to carry the luggage to the car did she realize she hadn't included anything for herself. The thought of having to choose a dress to wear at her own father's funeral nearly undid her. Unable to make a decision, she ended up stuffing every decent thing she owned into a suitcase.

"We can leave as soon as Glen and Ellie get here," Cal said, coming into the house for her bag.

"The roast," she said, remembering it was still in the oven.

"Don't worry about it. Glen and Ellie are on their way over. They'll take care of everything— they'll look after the place until we're back."

"Paul and Mary Ann?" The deep pain and re-sulting numbness refused to go away, and she was incapable of thinking or acting without being directed by someone else.

''They're fine, honey. I'll get them dressed and ready to go.''

She looked at her husband, and to her surprise felt nothing. Only a few minutes earlier she'd been convinced she was about to lose him to another woman. Right now, it didn't matter. Right now, she couldn't dredge up a single shred of feeling for Cal. Everything, even the love she felt for her husband, had been overshadowed by the grief she felt at her father's death.

Cal did everything he could to help Jane, her younger brother and Jane's mother with the funeral arrangements. Jane was in a stupor most of the first day. Her mother was in even worse shape. The day of the funeral Stephanie Dickinson had to be given a sedative.

Paul had been too young to remember Cal's mother, and Cal doubted Mary Ann would recall much of grandpa Dickinson, either. All the children knew was that something had happened that made their mother and grandmother cry. They didn't understand what Cal meant when he explained that their grandfather had died.

The funeral was well attended, as was the reception that followed. Harry Dickinson had been liked and respected. Cal admired the way Jane stepped in and handled the social formalities. Her mother just couldn't do it, and her brother Derek, seemed trapped in his own private pain and wasn't much good to anyone.

Only later, after everyone had left, did he find his wife sitting in the darkened kitchen. Cal sat at the table beside her, but when he reached for her, she stiffened. Not wanting to upset her, he removed his hand from her arm.

"You must be exhausted," he said. "When was the last time you ate?"

"I just buried my father, Cal. I don't have much of an appetite."

"Honey—"

"I need a few minutes alone, please."

Cal nodded, then stood up and left the room. The house was dark, the children asleep, but the thought of going to bed held no appeal. Sedated, his mother-in-law was in her room and his wife sat in the shadows.

The day he'd buried his own mother had been the worst of his life, Cal remembered. Jane had been by his side, his anchor. He didn't know how he could have survived without her. Yet now, with her father's death, she'd sent him away, asked for time alone. It felt like a rejection of him and his love, and dammit all, that hurt.

Everyone handled grief differently, he reminded himself. People don't know how they'll react until it happens to them, he reasoned. Sitting on the edge of the bed, he mulled over the events of the past few days. They were a blur in his mind.

His arms ached to hold Jane. He loved his wife, loved his children. Their marriage had been going through a rough time, but everything would work out, he was sure. Cal waited for Jane to come to bed, and when she didn't, he must have fallen asleep. He awoke around two in the morning and discovered he was alone. Still in his clothes, he got up and went in search of his wife.

She was sitting where he'd left her. "Jane?" he whispered, not wanting to startle her.

"What time is it?" she asked.

"Time for you to come to bed."

She responded with a shake of her head. "No. I can't."

"You've haven't slept in days."

"I know how long it's been," she snapped,

showing the first bit of life since that phone call with the terrible news.

"Honey, please! This is crazy, sitting out here like this. You haven't changed your clothes. This has been a hard day for you...."

She looked away, and in the room's faint light, he saw tears glistening on her face.

"I want to help you," he said urgently.

"Do you, Cal? Do you really?"

Her question shocked him. "You're my wife! Of course I do."

She started to sob then, and Cal was actually glad to see it. She needed to acknowledge her grief, to express it however she could. Other than when she'd first received the news, Jane had remained dry-eyed and strong. Her mother and brother were emotional wrecks, and her uncle Ken had been badly shaken. It was Jane who'd held them all together, Jane who'd made all the decisions and arrangements, Jane who'd seen to the guests and reassured family and friends. It was time for her to let go, time to grieve.

"Cry, honey. Let it out." He handed her a clean handkerchief.

She clutched it to her face, and sobbed more loudly.

"May I hold you?"

"No. Just leave me alone."

Cal squatted down in front of her. "I'm afraid I can't do that. I want to help you," he said again. "Let me do that, all right?"

She shook her head.

"At least come to bed," he pleaded. She didn't resist when he clasped her by the forearms and drew her to her feet. Her legs must have gone numb from sitting there so long because she leaned heavily against him as he led her into the bedroom.

While she undressed, Cal turned back the covers.

She seemed to be having trouble unfastening the large buttons of her tailored jacket. Brushing her hands aside, Cal unbuttoned it and helped take it off. When she was naked, he pulled the nightgown over her head, then brought her arms through the sleeves. He lowered her onto the bed and covered her with the blankets.

She must have gone to sleep immediately. At least, that was what he thought.

As soon as he climbed into bed himself and switched off the light, she spoke.

"Cal, I'm not going back."

"Back? Where?"

"To Promise," she told him.

This made no sense. "Not going back to Promise?" he repeated.

"No."

"Why not?" he asked, his voice louder than he'd intended. He stretched out one arm to turn on the lamp again.

"I can't deal with all the stress in our marriage. Not after this."

"But, Jane, we'll settle everything...."

"She wants you."

At first he didn't realize that Jane was talking about Nicole Nelson. Even when he understood what she meant, it took a while to battle down the frustration and anger. "Are you saying she can have me?" he asked, figuring a light approach might help. It was definitely better than giving in to his anger.

"She's determined, you know—except you *don't* know. You don't believe me."

"Jane, for the love of God, think about what you're saying."

"I have thought about it. It's all I've thought about for days. You're more worried about me embarrassing you than what that woman's doing to us. I don't have the strength or the will to fight for you. Not after today."

Patience wasn't his strong suit, but Cal knew he had to give her some time and distance, not force her to resume their normal life too quickly. "Let's talk about it later. Tomorrow morning."

"I won't feel any differently about this in the morning. I've already spoken to Uncle Ken."

For years her uncle had wanted Jane to join his medical practice, and had been bitterly disappointed when she'd chosen to stay in Texas, instead. "You're going to work for your uncle?"

"Temporarily."

Jane had arranged all this behind his back? Unable to hide his anger now, Cal tossed aside the sheet and vaulted out of the bed. "You might have said something to me first! What the hell were you thinking?"

"Thinking?" she repeated. "I'm thinking about a man who lied to me and misled me."

"I never lied to you," he declared. "Not once."

"It was a lie of omission. What I didn't know wouldn't hurt me, right? Well, guess what, Cal? It hurt and it hurt bad. I don't want to be in a marriage where my husband's more concerned about being embarrassed than he is about the gossip and ridicule he subjects me to."

He couldn't believe they were having this conversation. "You're not being logical."

"Oh, yes, I am."

Cal stormed to one end of the bedroom and stood there, not knowing what to do.

"You'll notice that even now, even when you know how I feel, you haven't once asked me to reconsider. Not once have you said you love me."

"You haven't exactly been proclaiming your love for me, either."

His words appeared to hit their mark, and she grew noticeably paler.

"Do you want me to leave right now?" he asked.

"I...I..." She floundered.

"No need to put it off," he said, letting his anger talk for him.

"You're right."

Cal jerked his suitcase out of the closet and crammed into it whatever clothes he could find. That didn't take long, although he gave Jane ample opportunity to talk him out of leaving, to say she hadn't really meant it.

Apparently she did.

Cal went into the bedroom where the children slept and kissed his daughter's soft cheek. He rested his hand on his son's shoulder, then abruptly turned away. A heaviness settled over his heart, and before he could surrender to the regret, he walked away.

Chapter 7

"I realize how hard this is on you," Jane's mother said. It was two weeks since the funeral. Two weeks since Jane had separated from her husband. Stephanie busied herself about the kitchen and avoided eye contact. "But, Jane, are you sure you did the right thing?" She pressed her lips together and concentrated on cleaning up the breakfast dishes. "Ken is delighted that you're going to work with him, and the children are adjusting just fine, but..."

"I'm getting my own apartment."

"I won't hear of it," her mother insisted. "If you're going through with this, I want you to stay here with me. I don't want you dealing with a move on top of everything else.

"Mother, it's very sweet of you, but you need your space, too."

"No..." Tears filled her eyes. "I don't want to live alone— I don't think I can. I never have, you know. Not in my entire life and...well, I realize I'm leaning on you, but I need you so desperately."

"Mother, I understand."

"It's not just that. I'm so worried about you and Cal."

"I know," Jane whispered. She tried not to think of him, or of the situation between them. There'd been no contact whatsoever. Cal had left in anger, and at the time she'd wanted him out of her life.

"Did you make an appointment with an attorney?" her mother asked.

Jane shook her head. It was just one more thing she'd delayed doing. One more thing she couldn't make a decision on. Most days she could barely manage to get out of bed and see to the needs of her children. Uncle Ken was eager to have her join the practice. He'd already discussed financial arrangements and suggested a date for her to start taking appointments—the first Monday in the new year. Jane had listened carefully to his plans; however, she'd felt numb and disoriented. This wasn't what she wanted, but everything had been put into motion and she didn't know how to stop it. Yet she had to support herself and the children. So far she hadn't needed money, but she would soon. Cal would send support, she was convinced of that. She lacked the courage to call him, though. She hated the thought of their first conversation being about money.

"You haven't heard from Cal, have you?" Her mother broke into her thoughts.

"No." His silence wasn't something Jane could ignore. She'd envisioned her husband coming back for her, proclaiming his love and vowing never to allow any woman to stand between him and his family. Disregarding Jane was bad enough, but the fact that he hadn't seen fit to contact the children made everything so much worse. It was as though he'd wiped every thought of his family from his mind.

Two months ago Jane assumed she had a near-perfect marriage. Now she was separated and living with her mother. Still, she believed that, if not for the death of her father, she'd be back in Texas right now. Eventually they would've reasoned out all this unpleasantness and discord; they would have rediscovered their love. Instead, in her pain and grief over the loss of her father, she'd sent Cal away.

She reminded herself that she didn't need to ask him twice. Cal had been just as eager to escape.

Nicole Nelson had won.

At any other time in her life Jane would have fought for her husband, but now she had neither the strength nor the emotional fortitude to do so. From all appearances, Cal had made his choice—and it wasn't her or the children.

"We should talk about Thanksgiving," her mother said. "It's next week...."

"Thanksgiving?" Jane hadn't even realized the holiday was so close.

"Ken and Jean asked us all to dinner. What do you think?"

Jane had noticed that her mother was having a hard time making decisions, too. "That would be nice," she said, not wanting to plan that far ahead. Even a week was too much. She couldn't bear to think about the holidays, especially Christmas.

The doorbell chimed and Jane answered it, grateful for the interruption. Facing the future, making plans—it was just too difficult. A parcel deliveryman stood with a box and a form for her to sign. Not until Jane closed the door did she see the label addressed to Paul in Cal's distinctive handwriting.

She carried the package into the bedroom, where her son sat putting together puzzles. He glanced up when she entered the room.

"It's from Daddy," she said, setting the box on the carpet.

Paul tore into the package with gusto and let out a squeal of delight when he found his favorite blanket. He bunched it up and hugged it to his chest, grinning hugely. Jane looked inside the box and found a short letter. She read it aloud.

Dear Paul,
I thought you might want to have your old friend with you. Give your little sister a hug from me.

Love,
Daddy

Jane swallowed around the lump in her throat. Cal's message in that letter was loud and clear. He'd asked Paul to hug Mary Ann, but not her.

Jane was on her own.

The post office fell silent when Cal stepped into the building. The Moorhouse sisters, Edwina and

Lily, stood at the counter, visiting with Caroline Weston, who was the wife of his best friend, as well as the local postmistress. Caroline had taken a leave of absence from her duties for the past few years, but had recently returned to her position.

When the three women saw Cal, the two retired schoolteachers pinched their lips together and stiffly drew themselves up.

"Good day, ladies," Cal said, touching the brim of his hat.

"Cal Patterson," Edwina said briskly. "I only wish you were in the fifth grade again so I could box your ears."

"How're you doing, Cal?" Caroline asked in a friendlier tone.

He didn't answer because anyone looking at him ought to be able to tell. He was miserable and getting more so every day. By now he'd fully expected his wife to come to her senses and return home. He missed her and he missed his kids. He barely ate, hadn't slept an entire night since he got back and was in a foul mood most of the time.

Inserting the key in his postal box, he opened the small door. He was about to collect his mail when he heard Caroline's voice from the post-office side of the box. "Cal?"

He reached for the stack of envelopes and flyers, then peered through. Sure enough, Caroline was looking straight at him.

"I just wanted you to know how sorry Grady and I are."

He nodded, rather than comment.

"Is there anything we can do?"

"Not a damn thing," he said curtly, wanting Caroline and everyone else, including the Moorhouse sisters, to know that his problems with Jane were his business...and hers. No one else's.

"Cal, listen—"

"I don't mean to be rude, but I'm in a hurry." Not waiting for her reply, Cal locked his postal box and left the building.

When he'd first returned from California, people had naturally assumed that Jane had stayed on with the children to help Mrs. Dickinson. Apparently news of the separation had leaked out after Annie called Jane at her mother's home. From that point forward, word had spread faster than a flash flood. What began as a simple fact became embellished with each retelling. Family and friends knew more about what was happening in his life than he did, Cal thought sardonically.

Only yesterday Glen had asked him about the

letter from Paul. Cal hadn't heard one word from his wife or children, but then he hadn't collected his mail, either. When Cal asked how Glen knew about any damn letter, his brother briskly informed him that Ellie had told him. Apparently Ellie had heard it from Dovie, and Dovie just happened to be in the post office when Caroline was sorting mail. This was life in a small town.

As soon as he stepped out of the post office, Cal quickly shuffled through the envelopes and found the letter addressed to him in Jane's familiar writing. The return address showed Paul's name.

Cal tore into the envelope with an eagerness he couldn't hide.

Dear Daddy,
Thank you for my blankey. I sleep better with it. Mary Ann likes it, too, and I sometimes share with her. Grandma still misses Grandpa. We're spending Thanksgiving with Uncle Ken and Aunt Jean.

Love,
Paul

Cal read the letter a second time, certain he was missing something. Surely there was a hidden message there from Jane, a subtle hint to let him know what she was thinking. Perhaps the mention of Thanksgiving was her way of telling him that she was proceeding with her life as a single woman. Her way of informing him that she was managing perfectly well without a husband.

Thanksgiving? Cal had to stop and think about the date, and he realized it'd been nearly three weeks since he'd last talked to Jane. Three weeks since he'd hugged his children. Three weeks that he'd been walking around in a haze of wounded pride and frustrated anger.

Not wanting to linger in town, Cal returned to the ranch. He looked at the calendar and was stunned to see that he'd nearly missed the holiday. Not that eating a big turkey dinner would have made any difference to him. Without his wife and his children, the day would be just like all the rest, empty and silent.

Thanksgiving Day Cal awoke with a sick feeling in the pit of his stomach. Glen had tried to talk him into joining his family. Ellie's mother and aunt were flying in from Chicago for the holiday week-end, he'd said, but Cal was certainly welcome. Cal declined without regrets.

He thought he just might avoid Thanksgiving

activities altogether, but should have known better. Around noon his father arrived. As soon as he saw the truck heading toward the house, Cal stepped onto the back porch to wait for him.

"What are you doing here, Dad?" he demanded, making sure his father understood that he didn't appreciate the intrusion.

"It's Thanksgiving."

"I know what day it is," Cal snapped.

"I thought I'd let you buy me dinner," Phil said blithely.

"I thought they served a big fancy meal at the seniors' center."

"They do, but I'd rather eat with you."

Cal would never admit it, but despite his avowals, he wanted the company.

"Where am I taking you?" he asked, coming down the concrete steps to meet Phil.

"Brewster."

Cal tipped back his hat to get a better look at his father. "Why?"

"The Rocky Creek Inn," Phil said. "What I hear, they cook a dinner fit to rival one of Dovie's Thanksgiving feasts."

"It's one of the priciest restaurants in the area,"

Cal muttered, remembering how his father had announced Cal would be footing the bill.

Phil laughed. "Hey, I'm retired. I can't afford a place as nice as the Rocky Creek Inn. Besides, I have something to tell you."

"Tell me here," Cal advised, certain his father had news about Jane and the children. If so, he wanted it right now.

Phil shook his head. "Later, son, later."

They decided to leave for Brewster after Cal changed clothes and shaved. His father made himself at home while he waited and Cal was grateful he didn't mention the condition of the house. When he returned wearing a clean, if wrinkled, shirt, and brand-new Wranglers, he found him reading Paul's letter, which lay on the kitchen table, along with three weeks' worth of unopened mail. He paused, expecting his father to lay into him about leaving his family behind in California, and was relieved when Phil didn't. No censure was necessary; Cal had called himself every kind of fool for what he'd done.

The drive into Brewster took almost two hours and was fairly relaxing. They discussed a number of topics, everything from politics to sports, but both avoided anything to do with Jane and the kids. A couple of times Cal could have led naturally into the subject of his wife, but didn't. No need to ruin the day with a litany of his woes.

The Rocky Creek Inn had a reputation for excellent food and equally good service. They ended up waiting thirty minutes for a table, but considering it was a holiday and they had no reservation, they felt that wasn't bad.

Both men ordered the traditional Thanksgiving feast and a glass of wine. Cal waited until the waiter had poured his chardonnay before he spoke. "You had something you wanted to tell me?" He'd bet the ranch that whatever it was had to involve the current situation with Jane. But he didn't mind. After three frustrating weeks, he hoped Phil had some news.

"Do you remember when I had my heart attack?"

Cal wasn't likely to forget. He'd nearly lost his father. "Of course."

"What you probably don't know is that your mother and I nearly split up afterward."

"You and Mom?" Cal couldn't hide his shock. As far as he knew, his parents' marriage had been rock-solid from the day of their wedding until they'd lowered his mother into the ground.

"I was still in the hospital recovering from the surgery and your mother, God bless her, waltzed into my room and casually announced that she'd put earnest money down on the old Howe place."

Cal reached for his wineglass in an effort to stifle a grin. He remembered the day vividly. The doctors had talked to the family following open-heart surgery and suggested Phil think about reducing his hours at the ranch. Shortly after that, his parents decided to open a bed-and-breakfast in town. It was then that Cal and his brother had taken over the operation of the Lonesome Coyote Ranch.

"Your mother didn't even *ask* me about buying that monstrosity," his father told him. "I was on my death bed—"

"You were in the hospital," Cal corrected.

"All right, all right, but you get the picture. Next thing I knew, Mary comes in and tells me, *tells* me, mind you, that I've retired and the two of us are moving to town and starting a bed-and-breakfast."

Cal nearly burst out laughing, although he was well aware of exactly what his mother had done and why. Getting Phil to cut back his hours would have been impossible, and Mary Patterson had realized that retirement would be a difficult adjustment for a man who'd worked cattle all his life. Phil wasn't capable of spending his days lazing around, so she'd taken matters into her own hands.

"I didn't appreciate what your mother did, manipulating me like that," Phil continued. "She knew I never would have agreed to living in town, and she went ahead and made the decision, anyway."

"But, Dad, it was a brilliant idea." The enterprise had been a money-maker from the first. The house was in fairly good condition, but had enough quirks to keep his father occupied with a variety of repair projects. The bed-and-breakfast employed the best of both his parents' skills. Phil was a natural organizer and his mother was personable and warm, good at making people feel welcome.

His father's eyes momentarily clouded. "It *was* brilliant, but at the time I didn't see it that way. I don't mind telling you I was mad enough to consider ending our marriage."

Cal frowned. "You didn't mean it, Dad."

"The hell I didn't. I would've done it, too, if I hadn't been tied down to that hospital bed. It gave me time to think about what I'd do without Mary in my life, and after a few days I decided to give your mother a second chance.''

Cal laughed outright.

''You think I'm joking, but I was serious and your mother knew it. When she left the hospital, she asked me to have my attorney contact hers. The way I felt right then, I swear I was determined to do it, Cal. I figured there are some things a man won't let a woman interfere with in life, and as far as I was concerned at that moment, Mary had crossed the line.''

Ah, so this was what Cal was supposed to hear. In her lack of trust, Jane had crossed the line with him, too; only, *he* hadn't been the one who'd decided to break up the family. That decision had rested entirely with Jane.

''I notice you haven't pried into my situation yet,'' Cal murmured.

''No, I haven't,'' Phil said. ''That's your business and Jane's. If you want out of the marriage, then that's up to you.''

''Out of the marriage!'' Cal shot back. ''Jane's the one who wants out. She decided not to return to Promise. The day of her father's funeral, she tells me she's staying with her mother... indefinitely.''

"You wanted this?"

"The hell I did!"

"But you left."

Cal had replayed that fateful night a hundred times, asking himself these same questions. Should he have stayed and reasoned it out with her? Should he have taken a stand and insisted she listen to reason? Three weeks later, he still didn't have the answer.

"Don't you think Jane might have been distraught over her father's death?" Phil wanted to know.

"Yeah," Cal agreed, "but it's been damn near a month now and she hasn't had a change of heart yet."

"No, she hasn't," Phil said, and sighed. "It's a shame, too, a real shame."

"I love her, Dad." Cal was willing to admit it. "I miss her and the kids." He thought of the day he'd found Paul's blankey. After all the distress that stupid blanket had caused him, Cal was so glad to see it that he'd hugged it to his chest, breathing in the familiar scent of his son. Afterward, the knot in his stomach was so tight he hadn't eaten for the rest of the day.

"I remember when Jennifer left you," Phil said,

growing melancholy, "just a couple of days before the wedding. You looked like someone had stabbed a knife straight through your gut. I knew you loved her, but you didn't go after her."

"Hell, no." Jennifer had made her decision.

"Pride wouldn't let you," Phil added. "In that case, I think it was probably for the best. I'm not convinced of it this time." His father shook his head. "I loved your mother, don't misunderstand me—it damn near killed me when she died—but as strong as my love for her was, we didn't have the perfect marriage. We argued, but we managed to work out our problems. I'm sure you'll resolve everything with Jane."

Cal hoped that was true, but he wasn't nearly as confident as his father.

"The key is communication," Phil said.

Cal held his father's look. "That's a little difficult when Jane's holed up halfway across the country. Besides, as I understand it, communication is a two-way street. Jane has to be willing to talk to me and she isn't."

"Have you made an effort to get in touch with her?"

He shook his head.

"That's what I thought."

"Go ahead and say it," Cal muttered. "You think I should go after Jane."

"Are you asking my opinion?" Phil asked.

"No, but you're going to give it to me, anyway."

"If Jane was my wife," Phil said, his eyes intent on Cal, "I'd go back for her and settle this once and for all. I wouldn't return to Promise without her. Are you willing to do that, son?"

Cal needed to think about it, and about all the things that had been said. "I don't know," he answered, being as honest as he knew how. "I just don't know."

Nicole Nelson arrived for work at Tumbleweed Books bright and early on the Friday morning following Thanksgiving Day. With the official start of the Christmas season upon them, the day was destined to be a busy one. She let herself in the back door, prepared to open the bookstore for Annie, who was leaving more and more of the responsibility to her, which proved—to Nicole's immense satisfaction—that Annie liked and trusted her.

Nicole had taken a calculated risk over Thanksgiving and lost. In the end she'd spent the holiday alone, even though she'd received two dinner invitations. Her plan had been to spend the day with Cal. She would've made sure he didn't feel threatened, would have couched her suggestion in compassionate terms—just two lonely people making it through the holiday. Unfortunately it hadn't turned out that way. She'd phoned the ranch house twice and there'd been no answer, which left her to wonder where he'd gone and who he'd been with.

Apparently the wife was out of the picture. That had been surprisingly easy. Jane Patterson didn't deserve her husband if she wasn't willing to fight for him. Most women did fight. Usually their attempts were just short of pathetic, but for reasons Nicole had yet to understand, men generally chose to stay with their wives.

Those who didn't...well, the truth was, Nicole quickly grew bored with them. It was different with Cal, had always been different. Never before had she shown her hand more blatantly than she had with Dr. Jane. Nicole almost felt sorry for her. Really, all she'd been doing was enlightening Jane about a few home truths. The woman didn't appreciate what she had if she was willing to let Cal go with barely a protest.

The phone rang. It wasn't even nine, the store didn't officially open for another hour, and already they were receiving calls.

"Tumbleweed Books," Nicole answered.

"Annie Porter, please." The voice sounded vaguely familiar.

"I'm sorry, Annie won't be in until ten."

"But I just phoned the house and Lucas told me she was at work."

"Then she should be here any minute." Playing a hunch, Nicole asked, "Is this Jane Patterson?"

The hesitation at the other end confirmed her suspicion. "Is this Nicole Nelson?"

"It is," Nicole said, then added with a hint of regret, "I'm sorry to hear about you and Cal."

There was a soft disbelieving laugh. "I doubt that. I'd appreciate it if you'd let Annie know I phoned."

"Of course. I understand your father recently passed away. I am sorry, Jane."

Jane paused, but thanked her.

"Annie was really upset about it. She seems fond of your family."

Another pause. "Please have her call when it's convenient."

"I will." Nicole felt the need to keep Jane on

the line. *Know your enemy,* she thought. "My friend Jennifer Healy was the one who broke off her engagement with Cal. Did you know that?"

The responding sigh told Nicole that Jane had grown impatient with her. "I remember hearing something along those lines."

"Cal didn't go after Jennifer, either."

"Either?" Jane repeated.

"Cal never said who wanted the separation— you or him. It's not something we talk about. But the fact that he hasn't sent for you says a great deal, don't you think?"

"What's happening between my husband and me is none of your damn business. Goodbye, Nicole." Her words were followed by a click and then a dial tone.

So Dr. Jane had hung up on her. That didn't come as a shock. If anything, it stimulated Nicole. She'd moved to Promise, determined to have Cal Patterson. Through the years, he'd never strayed far from her mind. She'd lost her fair share of married men to their wives, but that wasn't going to happen this time.

So far she'd been smart, played her cards right, and her patience had been rewarded. In three weeks, she'd only contacted Cal once and that was about a book order. Shortly after he'd returned from California alone, the town had been filled with speculation. The news excited Nicole. She'd planted the seeds, let gossip water Jane's doubts, trusting that time would eventually bring her hopes to fruition. With Jane still in California, Nicole couldn't help being curious about the status of the relationship, so she'd phoned to let him know the book Jane had ordered was in. Only Jane hadn't ordered any book....

Playing dumb, Nicole had offered to drop it off at the ranch, since she was headed in that direction anyway—or so she'd claimed. Cal declined, then suggested Annie mail it to Jane at her mother's address in California. Despite her effort to keep Cal talking, it hadn't worked. But he'd been in a hurry; he must've had things to do. And he probably felt a bit depressed about the deterioration of his marriage. After all, no man enjoyed failure. Well, she'd just have to comfort him, wouldn't she? She sensed that her opportunity would come soon.

It was always more difficult when there were children involved. In all honesty, Nicole didn't feel good about destroying a family. However, seeing just how easy it'd been to break up this marriage made her suspect that the relationship hadn't been all that secure in the first place.

She'd bide her time. It wouldn't be long now before Cal needed someone to turn to. And Nicole had every intention of being that someone.

After speaking to that horrible woman, Jane felt wretched. With little effort, Nicole had let it be known that she and Cal were continuing to see one another. Sick to her stomach, Jane headed for her bedroom.

"Jane." Her mother stepped into the room. "Are you all right? Was that Cal on the phone? What happened? I saw you talking and all at once the color drained from your face and you practically ran in here."

"I'm fine, Mom," Jane assured her. "No, it wasn't Cal. It wasn't anyone important."

"I finished writing all the thank-you notes and decided I need a break. How about if I take you and the children out to lunch?"

The thought of food repelled her. "I don't feel up to going out, Mom. Sorry."

"You won't mind if I take the children? Santa's arriving at the mall this afternoon and I know Paul and Mary Ann will be thrilled."

An afternoon alone sounded wonderful to Jane. "Are you sure it won't be too much for you?"

"Time with these little ones is *exactly* what I need."

"Is there anything you want me to do while you're out?" Jane asked, although she longed for nothing more than a two-hour nap.

"As a matter of fact, there is," Stephanie said. "I want you to rest. You don't look well. You're tired and out of sorts."

That was putting it mildly. Jane felt devastated and full of despair, and given the chance, she'd delight in tearing Nicole Nelson's eyes out! What a lovely Christian thought, she chastised herself.

"Mom." Paul stood in the doorway to her bedroom.

"Aren't you going with Grandma?" Jane asked.

Paul nodded, then came into the room and handed her his blankey. "This is for you." Jane smiled as he placed the tattered much-loved quilt on the bed.

"Thank you, sweetheart," she said, and kissed his brow.

Jane heard the front door close as the children left with her mother. Taking them to a mall the day after Thanksgiving was the act of an insane woman, in Jane's opinion. She wouldn't be caught anywhere near crowds like that. As soon as the thought formed in her mind, Jane realized she hadn't always felt that way. A few years ago she'd been just as eager as all those other shoppers. Even in medical school she'd found time to hunt down the best buys. It'd been a matter of pride; the cheaper she could purchase an item, the bigger the bragging rights.

Not so these days. None of that seemed important anymore. The closest mall was a hundred miles from the ranch. Most everything she owned was either bought in town or ordered through a catalog or over the Internet. The life she lived now was based in small-town America. And she loved it.

She missed Promise. She missed her husband even more.

Her friends, too. Jane could hardly imagine what they must think. The only person she'd talked to had been Annie, and then just once and briefly. Annie had called the week before. When she asked about Cal, Jane had refused to discuss him, other than to say they'd separated. It would do no good to rehash her current situation with Annie, especially since Nicole worked for her now.

With her son's blanket wrapped around her shoulders, Jane did manage to sleep for an hour. When she awoke, she knew instantly who she needed to talk to—Dovie Hennessey.

The older woman had been her first friend in Promise, and Jane valued her opinion. Maybe Dovie could help her muddle her way through the events of the past few months. She was sorry she hadn't talked to her earlier. She supposed it was because her father's death had shaken her so badly; she'd found it too difficult to reach out. Dealing with the children depleted what energy she had. Anything beyond the most mundane everyday functions seemed beyond her. As a physician, Jane should have recognized the signs of depression earlier, but then, it was often much harder to be objective about one's own situation.

To her disappointment Dovie didn't answer. She could have left a message on the answering machine, but she didn't. Briefly she considered calling her husband, but she didn't have the courage yet. What would she say? What would *he* say? If Nicole answered, it would destroy her, and just now Jane felt too fragile to deal with that kind of betrayal.

Her mother was an excellent housekeeper, but

Jane went around picking up toys and straightening magazines, anything to keep herself occupied. The mail was on the counter and Jane saw that it contained a number of sympathy cards. She read each one, which renewed her overwhelming sense of loss and left her in tears.

Inside one of the sympathy cards was a letter addressed to her mother. Jane didn't read it, although when she returned it to the envelope, she saw the name. Laurie Jo. Her mother's best friend from high school. Laurie Jo Spencer was the kind of friend to her mother that Annie had always been to Jane. Lately, though, with Annie so busy dealing with the changes in her own life, they hadn't talked nearly as much, Jane reflected sadly.

Laurie Jo had added a postscript asking Stephanie to join her in Mexico over the Christmas holidays. They were both recent widows, as well as old friends; they'd be perfect companions for each other.

Jane wondered if her mother would seriously consider such a trip and hoped she would. It sounded ideal. Her father's health problems had started months ago, and he'd required constant attention and care. Stephanie was physically and emotionally worn out.

If her mother did take the trip, it'd be the perfect time for Jane to find her own apartment. That way, her moving out would cause less of a strain in their relationship. To this point, Stephanie had insisted Jane stay with her.

In another four weeks it'd be Christmas. Jane would have to make some decisions before then. Painful decisions that would force her to confront realities she'd rather not face. This lack of energy and ambition, living one day to the next, allowing others to lead her, was beginning to feel like the norm. Beginning to feel almost comfortable. But for her own sake and the sake of her children, it couldn't continue.

Jane glanced at the phone again. She dialed Dovie's number, but there was still no answer.

She didn't leave a message. It occurred to her that Dovie's absence was really rather symbolic. There didn't seem to be anyone or anything left for her in Promise, Texas.

Chapter 8

Cal had never been much of a drinking man. An occasional beer, wine with dinner, but he rarely broke into the hard stuff. Nor did he often drink alone. But after six weeks without his family, Cal was considering doing both. The walls felt like they were closing in on him. Needing to escape and not welcoming company, Cal drove into Promise and headed straight for Billy D's, the local watering hole.

The Christmas lights were up, Cal noticed when he hit Main Street. Decorations were everywhere—in store windows and displayed on every lamppost. Huge red-and-white-striped candy canes and large wreaths dangled from the streetlights. Everything around town looked disgustingly cheerful, which only served to depress him further. He'd never been a Christmas nut, but Jane was as bad as his mother. A year ago Jane had decided to make ornaments for everyone in the family. She'd spent hours pinning brightly colored beads to red satin balls, each design different, each ornament unique. Even Cal had to admit they were works of art. His wife's talent had amazed him, but she'd shrugged off his praise, claiming it was something she'd always planned to do.

Last Christmas, Paul hadn't quite understood what Christmas was all about, but he'd gotten into the spirit of it soon enough. Seeing the festivities through his son's eyes had made the holidays Cal's best ever. This year would be even better now that both children—the thought pulled him up short. Without Jane and his family, this Christmas was going to be the worst of his life.

Cal parked his truck outside the tavern and sat there for several minutes before venturing inside. The noise level momentarily lessened when he walked in as people noted his arrival, but then quickly resumed. Wanting to be alone, Cal chose a table at the back of the room, and as soon as the waitress appeared, he ordered a beer. Then another and another.

He must have been there an hour, perhaps longer, when an attractive woman made her way toward him and stood, hands on her shapely hips, directly in front of his table.

"Hello, Cal."

It was Nicole Nelson. Cal stiffened with dread, since it was this very woman who had been responsible for most of his problems.

"Aren't you going to say it's nice to see me?"

"No."

She wore skin-tight jeans, a cropped beaded top and a white Stetson. At another time he might have thought her attractive, but not in his present frame of mind.

"Mind if I join you?"

He was about to explain that he'd rather drink alone, but apparently she didn't need an invitation to pull out a chair and sit down. He seemed to remember she'd done much the same thing the night she'd found him at the Mexican Lindo. The woman did what *she* wanted, regardless of other people's preferences and desires. He'd never liked that kind of behavior and didn't understand why he tolerated it now.

"I'm sorry to hear about you and Jane."

His marriage was the last subject he intended to discuss with another woman, especially Nicole. He didn't respond.

"You must be lonely," she went on.

He shrugged and reached for his beer, taking a healthy swallow.

"I think it's a good idea for you to get out, mingle with friends, let the world know you're your own man."

She wasn't making a damn bit of sense to Cal. He figured she'd leave as soon as she understood that he wasn't going to be manipulated into a conversation.

"The holidays are a terrible time to be alone," she said, leaning forward with her elbows on the table. She propped her chin in her hands. "It's hard. I know."

Cal took another swallow of beer. She'd get the message soon enough. At least he hoped she would.

"I always thought you and I had a lot in common," she continued.

Unable to suppress his reaction, he arched his eyebrows. She leaped on that as if he'd talked nonstop for the past ten minutes.

"It's true Cal. Look at us. We're both killing a Saturday night in a tavern, simply because we don't have anyplace better to go. We struggle to hold in our troubles for fear anyone will know the real us.''

The woman was so full of malarkey it was all Cal could do not to laugh in her face.

''I can help you through this,'' she said earnestly.

''Help me?'' He shouldn't have spoken, but he couldn't imagine what Nicole had to offer that could possibly interest him.

''I made a terrible mistake before, when Jennifer broke off the engagement. You needed me then, but I was too young to realize it, too young to know what I could do. I'm woman enough to have figured it out now.''

''Really?'' This entire conversation was laughable.

Her smile was coy. ''You want me, Cal,'' she said boldly, her unwavering gaze holding him captive. ''That's good, because I want you, too. I've always wanted you.''

''I'm married, Nicole.'' That was a little matter she'd conveniently forgotten.

''Separated,'' she corrected.

This woman had played no small part in that separation, and Cal was seeing her with fresh eyes.

''It'd be a good idea if you left,'' he said, not

bothering to mince words. Until now, Cal had assumed Jane was being paranoid about Nicole Nelson. Yes, they'd bumped into each other at the Mexican Lindo. Yes, she'd baked him a casserole and delivered it to the house. Both occasions meant zilch to him. Until today, he'd believed that Jane had overreacted, that she'd been unreasonable. But at this moment, everything Jane had said added up in his mind, along with his stubborn denial.

"Leave?" She pouted prettily. "You don't mean that."

"Nicole, I'm married and I happen to love my wife and children very much. I'm not interested in a dalliance with you or anyone else."

"I...I hope you don't think that's what I was saying." She revealed the perfect amount of confusion.

"I know exactly what you were saying. What else is this 'I want you' business? You're right about one thing though—I know what I want and, frankly, it isn't you."

"Cal," she whispered shaking her head. "I'm sure you misunderstood me."

He snickered softly.

"You're looking for company," she said, "otherwise you would've drunk your beer at home. I understand that, because I know what it's like to be alone, to want to connect with someone, anyone. Your thoughts are oppressive and you want someone with a willing ear.''

Cal had any number of family and friends with whom he could discuss his woes, and he doubted Nicole had any viable solutions to offer. He groaned. Sure as hell, Jane would get wind of this encounter and consider it grounds for divorce.

''All right,'' Nicole said, and pushed back her chair. ''I understand this is a difficult time. Separation's hard on a man, but eventually you'll want to talk about this. I'll be there, for you, okay? Call me. I'll wait to hear from you.''

As far as Cal was concerned, Nicole would have a very long wait. He settled his tab, and then, because he didn't want to drive, he walked over to the café in the bowling alley.

''You want some food to go with that coffee?'' Denise asked pointedly.

''I guess,'' he muttered, realizing he hadn't eaten much of anything in days. ''Bring me whatever you want. I don't care.''

Five minutes later she returned with a plate of corned-beef hash, three fried eggs, plus hash browns and a thick stack of sourdough toast.

"That's breakfast," he said, looking down at the plate.

"I figured it was your first decent meal of the day."

"Well, yeah." It was.

Denise set the glass coffeepot on the table. "You okay?"

He nodded.

"You don't look it. We went all the way through school together, Cal, and I feel I can be honest with you. But don't worry— I'm not about to give you advice."

"Good." He'd had a confrontation with his brother earlier in the day about his marriage. Then he'd heard from Nicole. Now Denise. Everyone seemed to want to tell him what to do.

"I happen to think the world of Dr. Jane, and of you. So work it out before I lose faith in you."

"Yes, Denise," he muttered, picking up his fork.

Cal had just about finished his meal when Wade McMillen slipped into the booth across from him. "Hi, Cal. How're you doing?"

Cal scowled. This was the very reason he'd avoided coming into town. People naturally assumed he was looking for company and so had no compunction about offering him that, plus advice.

"Heard from Jane lately?" Wade asked.

Talk about getting straight to the point.

"No." Cal glared at the man who was both pastor and friend. At times it was hard to see the boundary between those two roles. "I don't remember inviting you to join me," he muttered and reached for the ketchup, smearing a glob on his corned-beef hash.

"You didn't."

"What is it with people?" Cal snapped. "Can't they leave me the hell alone?"

Wade chuckled. "That was an interesting choice of words. Leave you *the hell alone.* I imagine that's what it must feel like for you about now. Like you're in hell and all alone."

"What gives you that impression?" Cal dunked a slice of toast into the egg yolk, doing his best to appear unaffected.

"Why else would you come into town? You're going stir-crazy on that ranch without Jane and the kids."

"Listen, Wade," Cal said forcefully, "I wasn't the one who wanted a separation. Jane made that decision. I didn't want this. In fact, I didn't do a damn thing.''

His words were followed by silence. Then Wade said mildly, ''I'm sure that's true. You didn't do a damn thing.''

Cal met his gaze. ''What do you mean by that?''

''That, my friend, is for you to figure out.'' Wade stood up and left the booth.

For the tenth time that day, Dovie Hennessey found herself staring at the telephone, willing it to ring, willing Jane Patterson to call from California.

''You're going to do it, aren't you?'' Frank said, his voice muted from behind the morning paper. ''Despite everything you said earlier, you're going to contact Jane.''

''I don't know what I'm going to do,'' Dovie replied, although she could feel her resolve weakening more each day. When she realized that Cal and Jane had separated, Dovie's first impulse had been to call Jane. For weeks now, she'd resisted. After all, Jane was with her mother and certainly didn't need advice from Dovie. If and when she wanted it, Jane would phone her.

Everything was complicated by Harry Dickinson's death. Jane was grieving, and Dovie didn't want to intrude on this private family time. First her father and then her marriage. Her friend was suffering, but she'd hoped that Jane would eventually make the effort to get in touch with her. She hadn't, and Dovie was growing impatient.

Few people had seen Cal, and those who did claimed he walked around in a state of perpetual anger. That sounded exactly like Cal, who wouldn't take kindly to others involving themselves in his affairs.

Dovie remembered what Cal had been like after his broken engagement. He'd rarely come into town, and when he did, he settled his business quickly and was gone. He'd been unsociable, unresponsive, impossible to talk to. Falling in love with Jane had changed him. Marrying Dr. Texas had been the best thing that had ever happened to him, and Dovie recalled nostalgically how pleased Mary had been when her oldest son had announced his engagement.

"Go ahead," Frank said after a moment. "Call her."

"Do you really think I should?" Even now Dovie was uncertain.

"We had two hang-ups recently. Those might have been from Jane."

"Frank, be reasonable," Dovie said, laughing lightly. "Not everyone's comfortable leaving messages on answering machines."

"You could always ask her," he said, giving Dovie a perfectly reasonable excuse to call.

"I could, couldn't I?" Then, needing no more incentive, she reached for the phone and the pad next to it and dialed the long-distance number Annie Porter had given her.

On the third ring Jane answered.

"Jane, it's Dovie—Dovie Hennessey," she added in case the dear girl was so distraught she'd forgotten her.

"Hello, Dovie," Jane said, sounding calm and confident.

"How are you?" Dovie cried, unnerved by the lack of emotion in her friend. "What about the children?"

"We're all doing fine."

"Your mother?"

Jane sighed, showing the first sign of emotion. "She's adjusting, but it's difficult."

"I know, dear. I remember how excruciating everything was for me those first few months after Marvin died. Give your mother my best, won't you?"

"Of course." Jane hesitated then asked, "How's everyone in Promise?"

Dovie smiled; it wasn't as hopeless as she'd feared. "By everyone, do you mean Cal?"

The hesitation was longer this time. "Yes, I suppose I do."

"Oh, Jane, he misses you so much. Every time I see that boy, it's all I can do not to hug him...."

"So he's been in town quite a bit recently." Jane's voice hardened ever so slightly. The implication was there without her having to say it.

"If that's your way of asking whether he's seeing Nicole Nelson, I can't really answer. However, my guess is he's not."

"You don't know that, though, do you? I...I spoke with Nicole myself and, according to her, they've been keeping each other company."

"Hogwash! What do you expect her to say? You and I both know she's after Cal."

"You know that?" Jane voice revealed strong emotion now.

"I didn't see it at first, but Frank did. He took one look at Nicole and said that woman was going to make trouble."

"Frank said that? Oh, Dovie, Cal thinks..."

Jane inhaled a shaky breath. Then she went quiet again. ''It doesn't matter anymore.''

''What do you mean? Of course it matters!''

''I made an appointment with a divorce attorney this morning.''

Stunned, Dovie gasped. ''Oh, Jane, no!'' This news was the last thing she'd wanted to hear.

''Cal's made his choice.''

''I don't believe that. You seem to be implying that he's chosen Nicole over you and the children, and Jane, that simply isn't so.''

''Dovie—''

''You said Nicole claimed she was seeing Cal. Just how trustworthy do you think this woman is?''

''Annie trusts her.''

''Oh, my dear, Annie hasn't got a clue what's happening. Do you seriously believe she'd stand by and let Nicole ruin your life if she knew what was going on? Right now all she's thinking about is this new pregnancy and the changes it'll bring about in *her* life. I love Annie, you know that. She's a darling girl, but she tends to see the best in everyone. Weren't you the one who told me about her first husband? You said everyone knew what kind of man he was—except for Annie. She just couldn't see it."

"I...I haven't discussed this with her."

"I can understand why. That's probably a good idea, the situation being what it is," Dovie said. "Now, let's get back to this business about the lawyer. Making an appointment—was that something you really wanted to do?"

"Actually my uncle Ken suggested I get some advice. He's right, you know. I should find out where I stand legally before I proceed."

"Proceed with what?"

"Getting my own apartment, joining my uncle's medical practice, and..." She let the rest fade.

"Filing for divorce," Dovie concluded for her.

"Yes." Jane's voice was almost inaudible.

"Is a divorce what you want?" Dovie couldn't believe that.

"I don't know anymore, Dovie. I just don't know. Cal and I have had plenty of disagreements over the years, but nothing like this."

"All marriages have ups and downs."

"I've been gone nearly six weeks and I haven't even heard from Cal. It's almost as...as if he's blotted me out of his life."

Dovie suspected that was exactly what he'd

been trying to do, but all the evidence suggested he hadn't been very successful. "What about you?" she asked. "Have you tried to reach him?"

Jane didn't want to answer; Dovie could tell from the length of time it took her to speak. "No."

"I see." Indeed she did. Two stubborn hurting people intent on proving how strong and independent they were. "What about the children? Do they miss their father?"

"Paul does the most. He asks about Cal nearly every day. Cal mailed him his blankey and...and he's taken to sucking his thumb again."

"And Mary Ann?"

"She's doing well. I don't think she realizes her father is out of the picture."

"You don't seriously believe that, do you?"

Jane breathed in deeply and Dovie realized she was holding back tears. "I can't tell anymore, Dovie. She's growing like a weed, and she looks so much like Cal."

"She deserves to know her father."

"And I deserve a husband."

"Exactly," Dovie said emphatically. "Then what are you doing seeing an attorney?"

"Cal will never do it. He'll be content to leave things as they are. He seems to think if he ignores me long enough, I'll come to my senses, as he puts it, and return home. But if I did that, I'm afraid everything would go back to the way it was before. My feelings wouldn't matter. He'd see himself as the long-suffering husband and me as a jealous shrew. No, Dovie, I'm not going to be the one to give in. Not this time.''

''So this is a battle of wills?''

''No, Dovie, it's much more than that.''

Dovie heard the tears in her voice, and her heart ached for Jane, Cal and those precious children. ''This is all because of Nicole Nelson,'' she said.

''Partially. But there's more.''

''There's always more,'' Dovie agreed.

''I guess Nicole crystallized certain...problems, or made them more evident, anyway.'' Jane paused. ''She as good as told me she wants him.''

That Dovie could believe. ''So, being the nice accommodating woman you are, you're just stepping aside and opening the door for her?''

This, too, seemed to unsettle Jane. After taking a moment to consider her answer, she said, ''Yes, I guess I am. You and everyone else seem to think I should fight for Cal, that I have too much grit to simply step aside. At one time I did, but just now… I don't. If she wants him and he wants her, then far be it from me to stand between them.''

''Oh, Jane, you don't mean that!''

''I do. I swear to you, Dovie, I mean every word.'' She stopped and Dovie heard her blowing her nose, then, ''I'm fine, sweetheart, go watch Mary Ann for me, all right?''

''That was Paul?'' Dovie asked. The thought of this little boy, separated from his father for reasons he didn't understand, brought tears to her eyes.

''Yes. He gave me a tissue.'' She took a deep breath. ''Dovie, I have to go now.''

''Sounds like you've made up your mind. You're keeping that appointment with the divorce attorney, then?''

''Yes. I'll be getting an apartment right after Christmas, and I'll move in at the first of the year.''

''You aren't willing to fight for Cal.''

''We've already been over this, Dovie. No, as far as I'm concerned, he's free to have Nicole if he wants, because he's made it quite plain he isn't interested in me.''

''Now, you listen, Jane Patterson. You're in too much emotional pain to deal with this right now. You've just lost your father. That's trauma enough without making a decision about your marriage. And isn't it time you thought about your children?''

''My children?''

''Ask yourself if they need their father and if he needs them. You won't have to dig deep to know the answers to those questions. Let them be your guide.''

To Dovie's surprise, Jane started to laugh. Not the bright humorous laughter she remembered but the soft knowing laughter of a woman who's conceding a point. ''You always could do that to me, Dovie.''

''Do what?''

Jane sniffled. ''Make me cry until I laugh!''

Cal knew something was wrong the minute Grady Weston pulled into the yard. The two men had been neighbors and best friends their entire lives. As kids, they'd discovered a ghost town called Bitter End, which had since become a major focus for the community. Along with Nell Bishop and the man she'd married, writer Travis Grant, they'd uncovered the secrets about the long-forgotten town. It was the original settlement— founded by Pattersons and Watsons, among others—and later re-established as Promise.

Grady jumped out of his pickup, and Cal saw that he had a bottle of whiskey in his hand.

"What's that for?" Cal asked, pointing at the bottle.

"I figured you were going to need it," Grady said. "Remember when I was thirteen and broke my arm?"

Cal nodded. They'd been out horseback riding, and Grady had taken a bad fall. Both boys had realized the bone was broken. Not knowing what to do and fearful of what would happen if he left his friend, Cal had ridden like a madman to get help.

"You recall when you brought my dad back with you, he had a bottle of whiskey?"

Cal nodded again. Grady's dad had given him a couple of slugs to numb the pain. It was at this point that Cal made the connection. "You've got something to tell me I'm not going to want to hear."

Grady moved onto the porch, and although it was chilly and the wind was up, the two of them sat there.

"I'm not getting involved in this business between you and Jane," Grady began. "That's your affair. Hell, I have my opinion, we all do, but what happens between the pair of you...well, you know what I mean.''

"Yeah."

"Savannah was in town the other day and she ran into Dovie."

No one needed to remind Cal what good friends Dovie and Jane were, had been for years. "Jane's talked to Dovie?"

"Apparently so."

"And whatever Jane told Dovie, she told Savannah and Savannah told Caroline and Caroline told you. So, what is it?"

Grady hesitated, as though he'd give anything not to be the one telling him this. "Jane's filing for divorce."

"The hell she is." Cal bolted upright, straight off the wicker chair. "That does it." He removed his hat and slapped it against his thigh. "Enough is enough. I've tried to be patient, wait this out, but I'm finished with that."

"Finished?"

"We start getting lawyers involved, and we'll end up hating each other, sure as anything."

Grady chuckled. "What are you going to do?"

"Do? What else? I'm going after her." He barreled into the house, ready to start packing.

"You're going to bring her home?" his friend asked, following him inside. The screen door slammed shut behind Grady.

"Damn straight I'm bringing her home. Divorce? That's just crazy!" So far, Cal had played it cool, let Jane have the distance she seemed to want and need. Obviously that wasn't working. He hadn't thought out his response to the situation, had merely reacted on an emotional level. In the beginning he was too damn mad to think clearly; his anger had quickly turned to bitterness, but that hadn't lasted long. Lately, all he'd been was miserable, and he'd had about as much misery as a man could take.

Grady gave him a grin and a thumbs-up. "Good. I wasn't keen on giving up my best bottle of bourbon, so if you have no objection, I'll take this back with me."

"You do that," Cal advised.

"Actually this is perfect."

"How do you mean?"

Grady laughed. "A Christmas reunion. Just the kind of thing that makes people feel all warm and fuzzy inside." The laughter died as Grady looked around the kitchen.

"What?" Cal asked, his mood greatly improved

now that he'd made his decision. He loved his wife, loved his children, and nothing was going to keep them apart any longer.

"Well..." Grady scratched his head. "You've got a bit of a mess here."

Cal saw the place with fresh eyes and realized he'd become careless again with Jane away. Their previous reunion had been tainted by a messy house. "I'd better do some cleaning before she gets home. She was none too happy about it the last time."

"You're on your own with this," Grady said, and headed out the door, taking his whiskey with him.

"Grady," Cal said, following him outside. His friend turned around. Cal was unsure how to say this other than right out. "Thank you."

Grady nodded, touched the brim of his hat and climbed into his truck.

Almost light-headed with relief, Cal returned to the kitchen and tackled the project with enthusiasm. He started a load of dishes, put away leftover food, took out the garbage, mopped the floor. He was scrubbing away at the counter when it occurred to him that after three weeks of caring for her parents, Jane must have been completely worn-out. Upon her return to Promise, she'd faced a gigantic mess. His mess.

Cal hadn't understood why she'd been so upset over a few dishes and some dirty laundry. He recalled the comments she'd made and finally understood them. What Jane had really been saying was that she'd wanted to be welcomed home for herself and not what she could do to make his life more comfortable. He'd left her with the wrong impression, hadn't communicated his love and respect.

He had to do more than just straighten up the place, Cal decided now. Glancing around, he could see plenty of areas that needed attention. Then it hit him—what Grady had said about a Christmas reunion. God willing, his family would be with him for the holidays, and when Jane and the children walked in that door, he wanted them to know they'd been on his thoughts every minute of every day they'd been apart.

Christmas. Jane was crazy about Christmas. She spent weeks decorating the house, and while he didn't have time for that, he could put up the tree. Jane and the kids would love that.

Hauling the necessary boxes down from the attic was no small task. He assembled the tree and set it in the very spot Jane had the year before. The lights were his least-favorite task, but he kept thinking of Jane as he wove the strands of tiny colored bulbs through the bright green limbs.

Several shoe boxes were carefully packed with the special beaded ornaments she'd made. He recalled the effort and time she'd put into each one and marveled anew at her skill and, even more, at the caring they expressed. In that moment, his love for her nearly overwhelmed him.

When he'd finished with the tree, he hung a wreath on the front door. All this activity had made him hungry, so he made himself a ham sandwich and ate it quickly. As he was putting everything back in the fridge—no point in undoing the work of the past few hours—he remembered his conversation with Wade McMillen a week earlier. Cal had stated vehemently that he hadn't ''done a damn thing,'' and Wade had said that was the problem. How right his friend had been.

This entire separation was of his own making. All his wife had needed was the reassurance of his love and his commitment to her and their marriage. Until now, he'd been quick to blame Jane, but he'd played an unsavory role in this farce, too.

Because of the holidays, he was forced to pay

an exorbitant price for a plane ticket to California the very next day, December twenty-second. Business class had the only seat available, and considering that he was plunking down as much for this trip as he would for a decent horse, he deserved to sit up front.

The next phone call wasn't as easy to make. He dialed his mother-in-law's number and waited through four interminable rings.

The answering machine came on. He listened to the message, taken aback when Harry Dickinson's voice greeted him. Poor Harry. Poor Stephanie.

He took a deep breath. "Jane, it's Cal. I love you. I love my children and I don't want to lose you. I'm on my way. I just bought a ticket and when I arrive, we can talk this out. I'll be there tomorrow. I'm willing to do whatever it takes to save our marriage and I mean that, Jane, with all my heart."

Chapter 9

"Dovie! Have you heard anything?" Ellie asked, making her way along the crowded street to get closer to Dovie and Frank Hennessey. She had Johnny by the hand and Robin in her stroller. Both children were bundled up in several layers of clothes to ward off the December cold.

The carolers stood on the opposite corner. Glen was with the tenors, and Amy McMillen, the pastor's wife, served as choral director. Carol-singing on the Saturday night before Christmas had become a tradition for Promise Christian Church since the year Wade married Amy. The event, naturally, was free of charge, but several large cardboard boxes were positioned in front of the choir to collect food and other donations for charity.

"I did talk to Jane," Dovie murmured for Ellie's ears only.

"Again?" Ellie asked, unable to hide her excitement.

Dovie nodded. "She's feeling very torn. I gather her mother's relying on her emotionally."

"But..."

"Don't worry, Ellie," Dovie whispered. "She's halfway home already. I can just feel it!"

"How do you mean?" Ellie was anxious to learn what she could. This episode between Cal and Jane had taken a toll on her own marriage. Glen was upset, so was she, and they'd recently had a heated argument over it, each of them taking sides. It seemed Cal and Jane's problems had seeped into their own marriage.

It'd all started when Ellie and Glen decorated the Christmas tree, and Ellie had found the beautiful beaded ornament Jane had made for her the previous year. She'd experienced a rush of deep sadness and regret, and she'd said something critical of Cal. Glen had instantly defended his brother.

She was baffled and disappointed by how quickly their argument had escalated. Within minutes, what had begun as a mere difference of opinion had become a shouting match. Not until later did Ellie realize that this was because they were so emotionally connected to Cal and Jane. She wasn't sure she could ever place that special ornament on the tree again and not feel a sense of loss, especially if the situation continued as it was.

"Did she keep the appointment with the attorney?" Ellie asked. The fact that Cal and Jane had allowed their disagreement to progress this far horrified her; at the same time it frightened her. Ellie had always viewed Cal and Jane's marriage as stable—like her own. If two people who loved each other could reach this tragic point so quickly, she had to wonder if the same sad future was in store for her and Glen.

The intensity of their own quarrel had shocked her, and only after their tempers had cooled were Ellie and Glen able to talk sensibly. Her husband insisted they had nothing to worry about, but Ellie still wondered.

Dovie shrugged. "I don't know what happened with the attorney. Doesn't Cal discuss these things with Glen?"

Ellie shook her head. "Cal won't, and every time Glen brings up the subject, they argue, especially in the last few weeks. When I told Glen about Jane seeing an attorney, he was furious."

"With Jane?"

"No, with Cal, but if Glen said anything to him, he didn't tell me."

"Oh, dear." Dovie wrapped her scarf around her neck.

The singing began and Ellie lifted Robin out of the stroller and held her up so the child could see her father. Johnny clapped with delight at the lively rendition of "Hark Go the Bells," and Robin imitated her brother.

Ellie's eyes met her husband's. Even though he stood across the street, she could feel his love and it warmed her. This entire ordeal of Cal's had been difficult for him. They both felt terrible that it had happened and, odd as it seemed, guilty, too. Ellie recognized this reaction for what it was, although she didn't know *why* they felt it. They had done nothing to cause the situation. Was it a kind of survivor guilt—that Cal and Jane's marriage was seriously threatened and theirs wasn't?

She wished now that she'd done something earlier, *said* something.

A warning about Nicole Nelson, maybe. A reassurance that this problem would pass. Anything.

"I have a good feeling," Dovie said, squeezing Ellie's arm. "In my heart of hearts, I don't think

Cal or Jane will ever let this reach the divorce courts.''

''I hope you're right,'' Ellie murmured, and shifted Robin from one side to the other.

The Christmas carols continued, joyful and festive, accompanied by a small group of musicians. The donation boxes were already filled to overflowing.

''You're bringing the children over for cookies and hot chocolate, aren't you?'' Dovie asked.

Ellie gave her a look that suggested she wouldn't dream of missing it. So many babies had been born in Promise recently, and several years ago, Dovie and Frank started holding their own Christmas party for all their friends' children. Dovie wore a Mrs. Claus outfit and Frank Hennessey made an appearance as Santa. Even Buttons, their poodle, got into the act, sporting a pair of stuffed reindeer antlers. For a couple who'd never had children of their own, Dovie and Frank did a marvelous job of entertaining the little ones.

''Johnny and Robin wouldn't miss it for the world,'' Ellie assured her. ''I just wish...''

Ellie knew what she was thinking. It was a shame that Paul and Mary Ann wouldn't be in Promise for the Hennesseys' get-together.

"I'm just as hopeful as you are that this will be resolved soon," Ellie said, forcing optimism in her words. She wanted so very badly to believe it, and she knew Dovie did, as well.

"Me, too," Nell Grant said, standing on the other side of Dovie. "The entire community is pulling for them." She blushed. "I hope you don't mind me jumping into the middle of your conversation."

"Everyone's hoping for the best," Dovie said with finality. Then, looking over at the small band of musicians, she turned back to Nell. "Don't tell me that's Jeremy playing the trumpet? It can't be!"

Nell nodded proudly. "He's quite talented, isn't he?"

"My goodness, look how tall he is."

"Emma, too," Nell said, pointing at the flute player.

"That's Emma?" Ellie asked, unable to hide her shock. Heavens, it'd only been a month or two since she'd last seen Nell's oldest daughter, and it looked as though she'd grown several inches.

With this realization came another. It'd been nearly six weeks since Cal had seen his children. At their ages, both were growing rapidly, changing all the time. She could only guess how much he'd missed—and felt sad that he'd let it happen.

Despite her disagreement with Glen, Ellie continued to blame Cal. Eventually he'd come to his senses, she knew, but she also hoped that when he did, it wouldn't be too late.

Her mother's mournful look tugged at Jane's heart as she finished packing her suitcase.

"You're sure this is what you want?" Stephanie Dickinson asked. Tears glistening in her eyes, she stood in the doorway of Jane's old bedroom.

"Yes, Mom. I love my husband. Things would never have gone this far if..."

"It's my fault, isn't it, honey?"

"Oh, Mom, don't even think such a thing." Jane moved away from the bed, where the suitcases lay open, and hugged her mother. "No one's to blame. Or if anyone is, I guess I am. I allowed everything to get out of control. I should have fought for my husband from the first. Cal was angry that I doubted him."

"But he—" Her mother stopped abruptly and bit her lip.

"You heard the message on the answering machine. He loves me and the children, and

Mom…until recently I didn't realize how *much* I love him. It's taken all this time for us both to see what we were doing. I love you and Uncle Ken, but Los Angeles isn't my home anymore. I love Promise. My friends are there, my home and my husband.''

Jane could tell that it was difficult for her mother to accept her decision. Stephanie gnawed on her lower lip and made an obvious effort not to weep openly.

''You talked to Cal? He knows you're coming?''

''I left a message on our answering machine.''

''But he hasn't returned your call?''

''No.'' There was such wonderful irony in the situation. Her mother had taken the children on an outing while Jane was scheduled to meet with the attorney. But as she'd sat in the waiting room, she'd tried to picture her life without Cal, without her family and friends in Promise, and the picture was bleak. She could barely keep from dissolving in tears right then and there.

Everything Dovie had said came back to her, and she'd known beyond a doubt that seeing this attorney was wrong. Paul and Mary Ann needed their father, and she desperately needed her husband. For the first time since her father's illness, Jane had felt a surge of hope, the desire to win back her husband. If Nicole thought Jane would simply walk away, she was wrong. At that moment, she'd resolved to fight for her marriage.

Without a word of explanation, Jane left the attorney's office and rushed home. The message light on the answering machine alerted her to a call, and when she pushed the button, Cal's deep voice greeted her. His beautiful loving voice, telling her the very things she'd longed to hear.

In her eagerness to return his call, her hand had shaken as she punched out the number. To her consternation she'd been forced to leave a message. Later phone calls went unanswered, as well. Her biggest fear was that he'd already boarded a plane, but she still hoped to detain him, and fly home with the children and meet him there. With that in mind, she'd booked her return flight.

"I'll try to reach him again."

"You could all spend Christmas here," her mother suggested hopefully.

"Mom, you're going with Laurie Jo to Mexico and that's the end of it."

"Yes, I know, but—"

''No buts, you're going. It's exactly what you need.''

''But your father hasn't even been gone two months.''

Jane shook her head sternly. ''Staying around here moping is the last thing Dad would want you to do.''

Her mother nodded. ''You're right...but I'm worried about you and the children.''

''Mom, you don't have to be. I know what I want.''

''But you can't go flying off without knowing if Cal will be there when you arrive!''

''I'll give Glen and Ellie a call. They'll make sure Cal gets the message and that someone's at the airport to get us.'' Jane sincerely hoped it would be Cal waiting when she stepped out of the jetway. This time she was sure their reunion would be everything their previous one wasn't.

Her mother frowned and glanced at her watch. ''You don't have much time. I really wish you weren't in such a rush.''

''Mother, I've been here nearly two months. One would think you'd be glad to get rid of me.'' This wasn't the most sensitive of comments, Jane realized when her mother's eyes filled with tears and she turned away, not wanting Jane to see.

"I shouldn't have depended on you and the children so much," Stephanie confessed. "I'm sorry, Jane."

"Mom, we've already been through this." She closed the largest of the suitcases, then hugged her mother again. "I'll call Ellie right now and that should settle everything. She'll make sure Cal knows which flight I'm on, or die trying."

She wished her husband would phone. Jane desperately wanted to speak to him, and every effort in the past three hours had met with failure. Funny, after all these weeks of no communication, she felt she'd burst if she didn't speak with him soon.

"Mommy, Mommy!" Paul raced into the bedroom and stuffed his blankey in the open suitcase. Then, looking very proud of himself, he smiled up at his mother. "We going home?"

"Home," she echoed, and knelt to hug her son. Her heart was full of such joy and anticipation it was all she could do to hold it inside.

Luckily, reaching Ellie wasn't difficult. Her sister-in-law was at the feed store and picked up on the second ring. "Frasier Feed," Ellie said in her no-nonsense businesswoman's tone of voice.

"Ellie, it's Jane."

"Jane!" Her sister-in-law nearly exploded with joy.

"I'm coming home."

"Hot damn, it's about time!"

"Listen," Jane said, "I haven't been able to get hold of Cal. He left a message that he's flying to California, but he didn't say when. Just that he's coming today."

"Cal phoned you?"

"I wasn't here. This is so crazy and wonderful. Ellie, I was sitting in the attorney's office and all of a sudden I knew there was no way I could go through with this. I belong with Cal in Promise."

"Whatever you need, I'll find a way to do it," Ellie promised. "You have no idea how much we've all missed you. None of us had any idea what to think when we didn't hear from you."

"I know. I'm so sorry. It's just that..." Jane wasn't sure how to explain why she hadn't called anyone in Promise for all those weeks. Well, she'd tried to reach Dovie, but—

"Don't apologize. I remember what it was like after my father died. One night I sat and watched old videos I knew he loved and I just wept. Even now I can't watch a John Wayne movie and not think of my dad.''

"You'll make sure Cal doesn't leave Promise?'' That was Jane's biggest concern. She hated the thought of arriving home and learning he was on his way to California. If that did happen, he'd find an empty house, because her mother was leaving, too.

"You can count on it.''

"And here, write down my flight information and give it to Cal—if you catch him in time.''

"I'll find him for you, don't you worry.''

Jane knew her sister-in-law would come through.

Cal spent the morning completing what chores he could, getting ready to leave. Glen was attending a cattlemen's conference in Dallas and would be home that evening, but by then Cal would be gone.

Now that his decision was made, he wondered what had taken him so long to own up to the truth. His love for Jane and their children mattered more than anything else—more than pride and more than righteousness. His friends and family had tried to show him that, but Cal hadn't truly grasped it until he learned how close he was to losing everything that gave his life meaning.

His father had urged him to listen to reason with that conversation during Thanksgiving dinner, and Phil's advice hadn't come cheap. Not when Cal was paying the bill at the Rocky Creek Inn.

Glen had put in his two cents' worth, too, and his comments had created a strain in their relationship. Cal couldn't listen to his younger brother, couldn't accept his judgment or his advice—although he wished he was more like Glen, easygoing and quick to forgive.

Even Wade McMillen had felt obliged to confront Cal. Every single thing his friends and family said had eventually hit home, but the full impact hadn't been made until the night Cal had gone to Billy D's.

Only when Nicole Nelson had approached his table had he seen the situation clearly. He'd been such a fool, and he'd nearly fallen in with her schemes. His wife was right: Nicole *did* want him. Damned if he knew why. It still bothered him that Jane hadn't trusted him, that she'd even suspect him of wanting another woman. He hadn't even been tempted by Nicole, he could say that in all honesty, but he'd allowed her to flatter him.

Cal had made his share of mistakes and was more than willing to admit it. He regretted the things he'd said and done at a time when Jane had been weakest and most vulnerable. Thinking over the past few months, Cal viewed them as wasted. He wanted to kick himself for waiting so long to go after his family.

As he headed toward the house, he saw Grady's truck come barreling down the driveway. His neighbor eased to a stop near Cal, rolled down his window and shouted, "Call Ellie!"

"Ellie? What about?"

"Hell if I know. Caroline called from town with the message."

"All right," he said, hurrying into the house.

Grady left, shouting "Merry Christmas" as his truck rumbled back down the drive.

When Cal reached his front door, he saw a large piece of paper taped there. "CALL ELLIE IMMEDIATELY," it read. "Good Luck, Nell and Travis."

What the hell? Cal walked into the house and immediately grabbed the phone. He noticed the blinking message light, but not wanting to be distracted, he ignored it.

"Is that you, Cal?" Ellie asked, answering the phone herself.

"Who else are you expecting?"

"No one."

She sounded mighty cheerful.

"You doing anything just now?" his sister-in-law asked.

"Yeah, as a matter of act, I am. I've got a plane to catch. It seems I have some unfinished business in California."

He'd thought Ellie would shriek with delight or otherwise convey her approval, since she'd made her opinion of his actions quite clear.

But all she said was, "You're going after Jane?"

He'd be on his way this very minute if he wasn't being detained. He said as much, although he tried to be polite about it. "What's all the urgency? Why is it so important that I call you?"

"Don't go!"

"What?" For a moment Cal was certain he'd misunderstood.

"You heard me. Don't go," Ellie repeated, "because Jane and the kids are on their way home."

"If this is a joke, Ellie, I swear to you—"

She laughed and didn't allow him to finish.

"When was the last time you listened to your answering machine?"

The flashing light condemned him for a fool. He should have realized Jane would try to reach him. In his eagerness he'd overlooked the obvious.

"What flight? When does she land?" He'd be there to meet her and the children with flowers and chocolates and whatever else Dovie could recommend. Ah yes, Dovie. Someone else who'd been on his case. He smiled, remembering her less-than-subtle approach.

Ellie rattled off the flight number and the approximate time Jane and the children would land, and Cal scribbled down the information. "How was she able to get a flight so quickly?" With holiday travel, most flights were booked solid.

"I don't know. You'll need to ask Jane."

Cal didn't care what she'd had to pay; he wanted her home. And now that the time was so close, he could barely contain himself.

As soon as he finished with Ellie, Cal played back the messages on his answering machine. When he heard Jane's voice, his heart swelled with love. She'd gotten his message and he could hear her relief, her joy and her love—the same emotions he was experiencing.

With his steps ten times lighter than they'd been a mere twenty-four hours ago, Cal got into the car and drove to town. Before he left, though, he carefully surveyed the house, making sure everything was perfect for Jane and the children. The Christmas tree looked lovely, and he'd even managed to buy and wrap a few gifts to put underneath. Not a single dirty dish could be seen. The laundry was done, and the sheets on the bed were fresh. This was about as good as it got.

Cal dropped in at Dovie's, then—because he couldn't resist—he walked over to Tumbleweed Books. Sure enough, Nicole was behind the counter. Her face brightened when he entered the store.

"Cal, hello," she said with an eagerness she didn't bother to disguise.

"Merry Christmas."

"You, too." People were busy wandering the aisles, but Nicole headed directly toward him. "It's wonderful to see you."

He forced a smile. "About our conversation the other night..."

Nicole placed her hand on his arm. "I was more blunt than I intended, but that's only because I know what it's like to be lonely, especially at Christmastime.''

''I'm here to thank you,'' Cal said, enjoying this.

Nicole flashed her baby blues at him with such adoration it was hard to maintain a straight face.

''You're right, I have been terribly lonely.''

''Not anymore, Cal, I'm here for you.''

''Actually,'' he said, removing her fingers from his forearm, ''it was after our conversation that I realized how much I miss my wife.''

''Your wife?'' Nicole's face fell.

''I phoned her and we've reconciled. You helped open my eyes to what's important.''

Nicole's mouth sagged open. ''I...I wish you and Jane the very best,'' she said, struggling to hide her disappointment. ''I should have known you'd go back to her.'' She shrugged. ''Most men do. It could have been good with us, Cal.''

Her audacity came as a shock. She'd actually believed he'd give up his wife and family for her. If he hadn't already figured out exactly the kind of woman she was and what she'd set out to do, he would have known in that instant. He should have listened to Jane—and just about everyone else.

"Stay out of my life, Nicole. Don't just happen to run into me again. Don't seek me out. Ever."

"You've completely misread the situation."

"That's what you said before." Cal shook his head. "But I don't think so."

"I'm sorry you feel this way."

During the course of his life, Cal had taken a lot of flack for being too direct and confrontational. Today he felt downright pleased at having imparted a few unadorned facts to a woman who badly needed to hear them. He walked out of the bookstore, and with a determination that couldn't be shaken, marched toward his parked car. He was going to collect his wife and children.

Jane's flight landed in San Antonio after midnight. Both children were asleep, and she didn't know if anyone would be at the gate to meet her. During the long hours on the plane, she'd fantasized about the reunion with her husband, but she'd begun to feel afraid that she'd been too optimistic.

All the passengers had disembarked by the time she gathered everything from the overhead bins and awakened Paul. The three-year-old rubbed his eyes, and Jane suspected he was still too dazed to understand that they were nearly home. Dragging his small backpack behind him, he started down the aisle. Mary Ann was asleep against her shoulder.

Jane's fear—that Cal might not be there—was realized when she came out of the jetway to find the area deserted. Her disappointment was so keen she stopped, clutching her son's hand while she tried to figure out what to do next.

"Jane...Jane!" Cal's voice caught her and she whirled around.

He stood at the information counter, wearing the biggest smile she'd ever seen. "I didn't know what to think when you didn't get off the plane with everyone else. I thought you—"

"This is your family?" the woman at the counter interrupted.

"Yes," he said happily.

Paul seemed to come fully awake then, and let out a yell loud enough to break the sound barrier. Dropping his backpack, the boy raced around the seating and hurled himself into Cal's waiting arms.

Cal wrapped his son in his embrace. Jane watched as his eyes drifted shut and he savored this hug from his son. Then Paul began to chatter until his words became indistinguishable.

"Just a minute, Paul," Cal said as he walked toward Jane.

With their children between them—Paul on his hip, Mary Ann asleep on her shoulder—Cal threw one arm around Jane and kissed her. It was the kind of deep open kiss the movies would once have banned. A kiss that illustrated everything his earlier phone message had already explained. A real kiss, intense and passionate and knee-shaking.

The tears of disappointment, which had been so near to the surface moments earlier, began to flow down her cheeks. But now they were tears of joy. She found she wasn't the least bit troubled about such an emotional display in the middle of a busy airport with strangers looking on.

"It's all right, honey," Cal whispered. He kissed her again, and she thought she saw tears in his eyes, too.

"I love you so much," she wept.

"Oh, honey, I love you, too. I'm sorry, so sorry."

"Me, too— I made so many mistakes."

"I've learned my lesson," he said solemnly.

"So have I. You're my home, where I live and breathe. Nothing is right without you."

"Oh, Jane," he whispered, and leaned his forehead against hers. "Let's go home."

They talked well into the night, almost nonstop, discussing one subject after another. Cal held her and begged her forgiveness while she sobbed in his arms. They talked about their mistakes and what they'd learned, and vowed never again to allow anyone—man, woman, child or beast—to come between them.

Afterward, exhausted though she was from the flight and the strain of the past months, Jane was too keyed up to sleep. Too happy and excited. Even after they'd answered all the questions, resolved their doubts and their differences, Jane had something else on her mind. When her husband reached for her, she went into his arms eagerly. Their kisses grew urgent, their need for each other explosive.

"Cal, Cal," she whispered, reluctantly breaking off the kiss.

"Yes?" He kissed her shoulder and her ear.

"I think you should know I stopped taking my birth-control pills."

Cal froze. "You what?"

She sighed and added, "I really couldn't see the point."

It was then that her husband chuckled. "In other words, there's a chance I might get you pregnant again?"

She kissed his stubborn wonderful jaw. "There's always a chance."

"How would you feel about having a third child?"

The way she felt just then, she'd be willing to give birth to triplets if it meant she could make love with her husband. "I think three children is a good number, don't you?"

"Oh, yes—and if it's a boy we'll name him after your father."

"Harry Patterson?" she asked, already picturing in her mind a little boy so like his father and older brother. "Dad would be pleased."

Two nights later, on Christmas Eve, Cal, Jane and the children drove into town to attend church services. Their appearance generated a good deal of interest from the community, Jane noted. Every head seemed to turn when they strolled into the church, and plenty of smiles were sent in their direction. People slipped out of their seats to hug Jane and slap Cal on the back or shake his hand.

When Wade stepped up to the pulpit, he glanced

straight at Cal, grinned knowingly and acknowledged him with a brief nod. Jane saw Cal return the gesture and nearly laughed out loud when Wade gave Cal a discreet thumbs-up.

"You talked to Wade?" she asked, whispering in his ear.

Her husband squeezed her hand and nodded.

"What did he say?"

"I'll tell you later."

"Tell me now," Jane insisted.

Cal sighed. "Let's just say the good pastor's words hit their mark."

"Oh?" She arched her brows and couldn't keep from smiling. Being here with her husband on Christmas Eve, sharing the music, the joy and love and celebration with her community, nearly overwhelmed her.

Not long after Jane and Cal had settled into the pew, Glen, Ellie and their two youngsters arrived, followed by her father-in-law. Phil's eyes met Jane's and he winked. Jane pressed her head to her husband's shoulder.

Cal slid his arm around her shoulders and reached for a hymnal, and they each held one side of the book. Organ music swirled around them, and together they raised their voices in song. "O,

Come All Ye Faithful.'' ''Silent Night.'' ''Angels We Have Heard on High.'' Songs celebrating a birth more than two thousand years ago. Songs celebrating a rebirth, a reunion, a renewal of their own love.

The service ended with a blast of exultation from the trumpet players, followed by the ''Hallelujah'' chorus from the choir. More than once during the service, Jane felt Cal's gaze on her. She smiled up at him, and as they gathered their children and started out of the church, she was sure she could feel her father's presence, as well.

Phil was waiting for them outside. Paul ran to his grandfather and Phil lifted the boy in his arms, hugging him.

''We have much to celebrate,'' he said quietly.

''Yes, Dad, we do,'' Cal agreed. He placed one arm around his father and the other around Jane, and they all headed for home.